COMHAIRLE CHONTAE ÁTHA CLIATH THEAS
SOUTH DUBLIN COUNTY LIBRARIES

LUCAN LIBRARY
TO RENEW ANY ITEM TEL: 621 6422

Items should be returned on or before the last date below. Fines, as displayed in the Library, will be charged on overdue items.

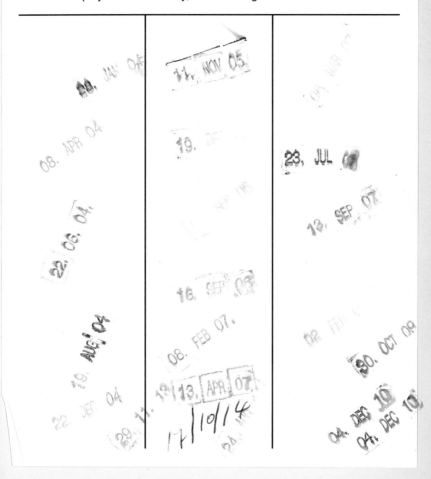

Also by Roderick Townley

The Great Good Thing

Into the Labyrinth

RODERICK TOWNLEY

SIMON &
SCHUSTER

SIMON &
SCHUSTER

First published in Great Britain by Simon & Schuster UK Ltd, 2003
A Viacom company

First published in 2002 by Atheneum Books for Young Readers,
an imprint of Simon & Schuster Children's Division, New York
Text copyright © 2002 by Roderick Townley

1 3 5 7 9 10 8 6 4 2

Simon & Schuster UK Ltd
Africa House
64-78 Kingsway
London WC2B 6AH

A CIP catalogue record for this book is available from the British Library

ISBN 0-689-83713-5

Printed and bound in Great Britain by The Bath Press, Bath

acknowledgments

Many thanks to Jack Rees, geometrician, for finding a shape for the book; and to Robin Prinzing and Eric Dinyer for making it compute. Thanks also to Amy Berkower for artful representation, Richard Jackson for incisive editing, Grace Townley for stellar suggestions and Wyatt Townley for, well, all of the above.

—R. T.

Again, for Wyatt and Grace

contents

part one • *web*

part two • *worpool*

part three • *paragon*

part one

Web

Chapter One

"She's about to jump!" shouted Riggeloff.

"Cree! Skricket!" cried the thieves, as they turned into insects.

"You're twelve years old," intoned the queen. "It's time to think of marriage!"

The voices echoed all around her, till sometimes the girl wanted to put her hands over her ears. Still, it was a delicious noise. Sylvie had an amazing life, and she got to live it dozens of times a day, now that the book she lived in was back in print.

Her life, in print again! For years, there had been one known copy of her story, and it sat on a shelf in the second-floor bedroom of an old house. But now, through what seemed a miracle, the book was republished, and Sylvie suddenly found herself in living rooms and waiting rooms, apartments, bus stations and the windows of bookshops.

Whatever a bookshop was. As far as she knew, *The Great Good Thing* was the only book in the world. Readers appeared above her with great regularity, their enormous faces peering down into her storybook world of villains and ladies-in-waiting, of spells and narrow escapes. The idea that they might also peer down into other stories never occurred to her. And if it hadn't occurred to *her,* it would never occur to her parents, king and queen of the realm, whose imaginations were limited to the words written for them. Finally it was Norbert Fangl, her tutor, who broke the news as they strolled one night by the Mere of Remind. A bony old fellow with sadly smiling eyes, Fangl was almost the only character in the story who was based on an actual person. In life he had been a geometry teacher, and he seemed to know everything, or could figure it out. Still, Sylvie didn't want to believe him.

"Does it disturb you, Princess," he said, "to think there might be other books?"

Sylvie thought. "It does. It's like being told there are other suns in the sky."

"There *are* other suns in the sky. Millions of them."

Sylvie laughed, her young cheeks bunching up. "Now you're making fun of me, Fangl."

He smiled kindly. "Am I going too fast?"

"You're not going fast, you're just talking silly."

"I'm sure you're right, Your Highness."

They continued along the curve of the shore, Sylvie doing a happy skip and not caring that mud was splashing her shoes. Tired though she was, she liked these midnight walks, when most Readers were asleep and the characters had time to themselves. The moon, always full, cast lines of wiggling silver over the water. Across the inlet lay the castle grounds with their woods and moonlit paths, and beyond them the dark turrets of the great structure itself. The distant moat gleamed weakly, sheeted with lilies, while over the whole scene drifted the delicious scent of newly printed pages.

"Although if there *are* other stories," said Sylvie, picking up the thread, "I'd like to know how the people in them deal with all these Readers. I hardly have time to catch my breath!"

"Most books are not as popular as *The Great Good Thing*."

"Really?" Sylvie felt pleased by the thought. "Really?" she said again. Her green eyes sparkled.

Just then a nearby bullfrog began a loud croaking. "Ooooopen!" it belched. "Booook oopen!"

"Isn't it a little late for people to be reading?" said Sylvie with a little puff of a sigh. "Oh well." She gave her tutor a quick wave and hurried towards page 5 of the new edition, where her dialogue with the king began.

"*Skraawk!*" cried an orange-and-white bird, taking off from a rock. "Reader!"

"I know, I know!" cried Princess Sylvie, racing down the narrow white path between lines of words. She arrived, panting a little, just as the moon and several clouds lifted away and a boy's face appeared overhead, backlit by a reading lamp.

"Father," Sylvie declared in a firm voice, "I cannot marry Prince Riggeloff."

The king's crown was crooked and he had a cross look on his face. Evidently, he'd been napping in the anteroom. "Not marry Riggeloff?" he grumped. "For Heaven's sake, child, he is handsome, rich . . ."

"Kind, brave," continued Princess Sylvie. "Yes, I am aware of his qualities."

So it went, Sylvie refusing to marry before she did one "great good thing" with her life, Prince Riggeloff's bitter reaction, his thieves' stealing the castle treasure, the invisible fish saving Sylvie when she leapt from the cliff, the horrid-looking Keeper of the Cave urging the princess to kiss the wound on his forehead. Fortunately, the Reader yawned loudly and let the book close before the start of Part Three. Part Three was the most demanding section of all.

The moon came back on again, full as ever.

"Who on Earth was that?" snapped Pingree the Jester, a short, spindly fellow with a face like a walnut.

"A ten year old, I believe," said Norbert Fangl, "from a place called Kansas."

"Don't they sleep in Kansas?"

"Just wait," replied Fangl. "When the Japanese translation is finished, we'll have Readers all through the night."

"Don't *they* sleep?"

"Difference in time zones. They sleep when other Readers are awake. It's fourteen hours later there."

Fangl noticed the other characters were staring at him. "It's simple, really. You see, the curve of the Earth . . ."

"Oh joy!" muttered Pingree. He swatted his jingling cap against his leg and set it at an angle on his head.

"We'll get no rest at all!" the queen faintly wailed.

Fangl looked about him in surprise.

Sylvie whispered, "I'm not sure you should have brought up all that about translations. Now they've got something else to worry about."

"Good thing I didn't mention the Urdu and Icelandic."

"Are we going to have to learn all those languages?"

"It seems not. You're already in several European languages and no one seems to have noticed."

"We *are?*"

"You think in whatever language you're written in."

"Fangl, you are full of surprises."

"Um, excuse me, old fellow," said King Walther, draping an arm around the old teacher's shoulder and drawing him aside. He gnawed on the end of his moustache, as he always did when he fretted. "Explain to me again about this time-zone business."

Slowly the characters drifted off, each in his own direction, to get a little rest before the day began and new Readers opened the book.

"Sylvie," hissed Queen Emmeline, when they were alone.

"Mother, are you all right? Your eyebrow is twitching."

The queen, she noticed, was wearing more make-up these days, to disguise her lack of sleep. "You've *got* to talk with the Writer. Get her to do something!"

"What's the matter?"

"The matter?" The queen closed her eyes and shook her head a fraction of an inch. "This jumping up and down every five minutes, that's what's the matter."

Sylvie put a calming hand on her mother's arm. "I know we've been pretty busy lately."

"Busy! My dear, a queen likes to sit on her throne and reign, not scamper about like a . . . like a . . . whatnot!" She picked up her little brown-and-white Chihuahua and patted its head. "Even Lulu is nervous."

"Lulu is always nervous."

"Yesterday she barked through my whole scene by the drawbridge."

"I'll see if I can talk to the Writer."

"If you do see her," the queen went on, "ask if she can do something about this awful gown. I don't know what's wrong with it; it just *hangs* on me."

"You've lost weight, Mother."

The queen raised an eyebrow doubtfully, then glanced in the looking glass at the trailing gown of green silk. "Do you suppose?"

"It's obvious."

"I've never lost an ounce before."

"You've never been so busy before. You should see Prince Riggeloff. With all his racing around, he's practically swimming in his clothes."

The queen considered this. "I was wondering what was different about him. He's always looked so snappy."

"It's hard to be snappy when you're tripping over your cape."

The queen gave one of her rare smiles. "He did trip, didn't he?"

"I'll talk to the Writer," continued Sylvie, "if I can get her attention."

"Thank you, child."

"Try to rest. Things will be starting up soon."

Queen Emmeline nodded, but she wasn't listening. She was looking in the mirror. "I can see why you're the heroine," she said, in better spirits. "You always see the bright side. And those lines of dialogue! I could never manage saying all that."

"You get used to it."

"I'm too old to get used to it." Cradling the squirming dog, she glided off to her chambers. Princess Sylvie watched her go. She'd promised that she'd speak to

Lily – that was the Writer's name – but meetings weren't easy to arrange. You couldn't just tilt your head back and shout. She had to wait till Lily had a dream that Sylvie could be part of. That happened less and less frequently, and Sylvie found it wise to make a list of things to bring up when they happened to be together.

"Mother frazzled," she scribbled. "Can she have fewer lines?" Then she wrote, "Alterations?" and slid the note into the pocket of her velvet dress.

The person she really wanted to talk to was the girl with the dark blue eyes. She always knew what to do. She might not be a whiz at logic, like Fangl, but she just knew things. Even the king consulted her. Where was she?

Sylvie stood fingering the gold locket that the girl had given her long ago. The princess clicked it open. There was her friend: the bright, almond-shaped face looking as if it could barely contain a secret, the suggestion of a smile playing about her small mouth. And those eyes, dark blue, undecided between mischief and mystery. Sylvie snapped the locket shut, absentmindedly rubbing the gold *S* on the lid.

The next day was busier than ever. It started with a librarian in Cleveland reading through most of Part

One faster than Sylvie had ever known Readers could read. Whoever librarians were, they sure could zip through a book! The characters kept up as best they could, but the king's knights were sweating as they raced around in heavy armour pursuing Riggeloff and his thieves. In the midst of this madness, a very young girl in Maine opened the book with soft fingers and began sounding out the words of Chapter One: "'Father,' said Princess Sylvie, 'I cannot marry Prince Rig . . . Rigga.' Mummy, what's this word?"

At about the same time, a boy waiting for a school bus in Hackensack, New Jersey, fished the book out of his backpack and started reading where he'd left off the night before. Unfortunately, it was raining in Hackensack that morning, and cold droplets kept plunking down in the bedchamber during Queen Emmeline's scene with Sylvie. Finally the school bus pulled up and the book was shoved into the backpack.

"Sylvie," the queen hissed, "you've *got* to talk to the Writer!"

"First chance I get, Mother."

"It's not just me. Everyone's miserable. We can't keep up this pace."

"I know, Mother."

"How can you be so cheery?"

"I guess I'm just happy to have a book to live in again. There were all those years when we didn't."

"I hardly remember. That time is vague to me."

Sylvie looked at her mother with surprise. It was all so *vivid*. "Surely you remember when that boy Ricky set fire to the book we were living in."

Queen Emmeline frowned and nodded. "I think so," she said slowly.

"Ricky. Claire's brother *Ricky*. He was trying to make the pages look old by burning the edges, but then the whole book caught fire."

"That's right, and we escaped somehow."

"We escaped into his sister's memory."

"Was she that unattractive little girl?"

"Claire was a wonderful friend and she saved us. I would never call her unattractive."

"My dear, she had a very wide mouth and mousy little curls."

"She kept us in her memory for years when we had no book to live in. And when she grew up, she told our story to her daughter, Lily."

"I'm not saying she wasn't a fine person."

"And when Lily grew up –"

"She wrote it down, yes. And here we are."

"Yes, Mother, here we are."

"A fine kettle of fish!"

Sylvie sighed. "Would you prefer the old days, when there was only one copy of the book and no one read us for ages at a time?"

"Much."

"Really?"

"Much-much-much."

Sylvie sighed. "Well, I'll talk to the Writer when I see her. Maybe she can cut back on your lines. But I can't promise."

As luck had it, Sylvie ran into the Writer that very night. Lily was not dreaming about the book exactly, but about something called a "talk show", which was to take place in a few days. From what Sylvie gathered from the dream, Lily was scheduled to discuss *The Great Good Thing* and how she had first heard the story from her mother, who had read it in a book *her* grandmother had owned decades before. Lily was always careful not to take credit for coming up with the plot.

Still, Lily admitted, it was gratifying to have an actual book in print and to see her own name on it. The money made a welcome change, too. Lily was able to buy a new computer to write on, and she immediately got herself hooked up to the Internet.

In the dream, Lily, looking pretty in a maroon trouser suit and cream-coloured blouse, was talking with a chuckling fellow with an upturned chin and his hair in a big, greying pompadour. The place didn't look a thing like the castle; there was not a turret or unicorn tapestry in sight. Instead of thrones, three chairs and a desk stood on a carpeted stage. Instead of armour, strange machines glided silently about, pointing first at the pleasant man with the puffy hair, then at Lily. This was one of Lily's Nervous Dreams, Sylvie realised, noticing numbers of brown mice nibbling at the gold fringe of the curtain and scooting along the backs of the chairs. One of the mice crept across the man's desk and stood on its hind legs to peer into his coffee cup.

When Lily was having one of her Nervous Dreams, you could never tell *what* might happen. Still, the man kept smiling. He spoke right at one of the gliding machines, and then leaned towards Lily confidingly.

"I just loved your invisible fish!" He chuckled and shook his head. "How did you come up with that one?"

Lily was smiling, but Sylvie saw the alarm in her eyes. "I didn't. Really!" A mouse poked its nose out of the sleeve of her blouse. Another crept up her neck. "That was just part of the story my mother told me." An electric saw backstage began screaming so loudly Lily couldn't hear herself speak.

"Look," she shouted over the hubbub, "here's Princess Sylvie now. She'll tell you!"

That was Sylvie's cue. A young assistant gave her a gentle shove, and she stepped onto the brightly lit platform while applause welled up around her. Sylvie was used to dreams, having appeared in enough of them in the past, so she threw herself into the part, happy to help Lily out, and especially happy to say lines that hadn't been pre-written for her. The sound of the power saw subsided, and the pleasant man invited Sylvie to take a seat – a much more comfy chair than those hard old thrones she usually perched on.

"We've never had a fictional character on the show before," he said with a smile. "Is it true you never get any older?"

"That's right. I've been twelve years old since 1917."

"I bet there are a lot of women in the audience who would like to know your secret!"

Laughter surged towards her from beyond the lights. He exchanged banter with her for several minutes, then looked into a gliding machine and said he would be

16

right back, although in fact he didn't go anywhere at all. Sylvie and Lily were the ones who had to get up and leave. That was all right; it was time for Lily to end this dream and start her day.

"Thanks," Lily whispered as they passed through the curtain into the backstage area. "You saved me."

"Glad to help. Say, before you wake up," said Sylvie, "there are a couple of things I wanted to ask." She told Lily about the ill-fitting costumes and the jumpiness and irritability of several characters, including the queen's dog.

"You mean they're stressed out?" said Lily.

"Dressed up?"

"No, stress. Haven't you heard of stress?"

"I don't think so. I've never seen one."

"It's what happens when you're too busy and you don't have time to do what you know you have to do."

"Oh!" said Sylvie as they opened a door and started down a long beige hallway. "Then I guess we do have stress. Lots."

"Let me think about this," said Lily. "Maybe I can come up with something."

"Will you remember when you wake up?"

"Of course I will! I'm about to wake up now."

"And the costumes?"

"We're going into a new edition. There were a bunch of mistakes in the old one, and we want to get them fixed before we're uploaded onto the Web."

"The what?"

"Isn't it exciting? We're going on-line! People will be able to read the book right off their computers."

"What are you talking about?" Sylvie knew about webs; she'd admired how pretty they could be when strung with dewdrops in the morning sun. But she also knew how sticky and sinister a web could be when its owner was at home.

"I forget," said Lily, "you probably don't have the Internet in your world. You don't even have computers! Anyway, we want to make the changes before the book's uploaded, and I'll see if the illustrator can make some alterations for you. Do you still like your colours?"

Sylvie stopped and looked at the Writer. "You're good to us."

"Well," said Lily, beaming, "I love you guys."

Sylvie gave Lily's hand a friendly squeeze. "The colours are fine," she said. "I guess it's just this stress business."

"I've got an idea about that. A friend of mine has been helping me deal with my own stress."

"You mean you've got one, too?"

"One stress?" Lily gave a laugh. "I've got more than one. But this person has helped me. She's younger than I am, but she knows all kinds of things. What would you think if I wrote her into the book?"

Sylvie stared. "You're not supposed to change the story."

"I know, I know." They had arrived at a bank of lifts at the end of the corridor. This was where Lily was to ride upstairs into the waking world.

"Can this person really help?" Sylvie pursued.

"She helped me."

"Oh yes, I could see how calm you were during tonight's dream!"

"Don't be sarcastic, Sylvie. You're not a sarcastic character."

"Well, is there some way you can do it so you don't change the story?"

"I'll think about it. What if I wrote her in but didn't give her any dialogue?"

Sylvie considered this.

"She could be a background character, a shepherdess

or something," Lily went on. "Then, when the book is closed . . ."

"She could help us. Oh, I like that!"

"Well, we'll see."

"Will you remember?"

"I said I would."

"Don't forget!" In fact, to be sure she didn't, Sylvie used her old trick of stepping hard on Lily's foot to make her wake up right away.

"Ow!"

"Go! Wake up!"

"All right, all right!"

The Writer stepped into the lift and the door closed. At the same moment, the hallway turned from beige to misty grey, then faded entirely, replaced by the faint lapping of water. Princess Sylvie found herself alone at daybreak, shivering beside the Mere of Remind.

Chapter Two

Sylvie loved her book. For all the adventures she underwent and dangers she faced, there was something soothing about the storyline. Everything would turn out well in the end. The villains would be vanquished. The kingdom would be saved. But there was one part she didn't care for. She wished there was a way to get around it or hurry over it; but she had to endure every fearful page of it.

That was the part where the princess tries to get the Keeper of the Cave to help her recover the stolen treasure. The old guardian of the cave was by far the creepiest character in the book. Sylvie couldn't understand why, time and again, Readers would return to the chapters where this gruesome old man stormed about his lair, screaming in anger and pain. It was as if Readers loved to get the shivers.

At first (as the story went), she didn't know how to find him. Rumour was that he lived somewhere within Humped Mountain, by the Mere of Remind, but how could she get inside a mountain? She found out one day as a result of a terrifying chase, when Prince Riggeloff's thieves nearly captured her in the forest. Ahead lay the cliff, and below, the dark waters of the Mere.

"She's about to jump!" shouted Riggeloff.

"Come on!" she yelled to her donkey. "Come on, little one, jump!"

They leaped into nothingness, sailed downwards for several endless seconds, and plunged into the Mere. Sylvie struggled to the surface, gasping, only to find arrows zinging all around her. She immediately dived under again. The arrows, stabbing the water, slowed and glided lazily past. Suddenly she felt herself being pulled down and realised with horror that she had been caught in the Mere's wandering whirlpool. Death waited above her, and death was pulling her below! Just then, the invisible fish – an enormous beast Sylvie had saved earlier in the book – swam over, opened its giant jaws and swallowed the girl whole!

Expelling the excess water from an opening in its back, the creature sank to the bottom, where Sylvie found herself with enough foul-smelling air to survive. She looked out its transparent sides at the passing rocks and weeds. Lantern fish left phosphorescent trails through the darkness.

It was in the gloomy depths of the Mere that Sylvie discovered the underwater entrance to Humped Mountain. The fish stopped at the place and slowly opened its jaws, letting the water rush in. At first, Sylvie was swept deeper into the fish's belly, but then the current swirled about and carried her out of the fish's mouth. Swimming strongly, she entered a cave-like opening in the rock. Darkness was total, but she felt herself rising through a narrow tunnel. Holding her breath became difficult, then unbearable. At last, when her lungs were near bursting, she broke through the surface, coughing and sputtering, to find herself in a cavern of some kind in the heart of the mountain. Looking up, she made out a dim light filtering from above. Her heart bumped in her chest as she pulled herself from the water and scrambled up a steep incline. Gradually the light grew more definite, and before long she reached the top, where the tunnel ended in a metal grate covered with bat droppings. Overcoming her disgust, she pushed it aside and climbed out into a room of stone. A wing flew past her head, then another. Bats were everywhere. A greenish light flittered all around her, and she realised it was coming from the walls themselves! The sides and ceiling of the room were encrusted with crystals.

"GET OUT!" boomed a frighteningly deep voice that bounced off the walls in crazy echoes. "GET OUT OF HERE!"

And that, as breathless Readers always found out on page 28, was Princess Sylvie's first encounter with the Keeper of the Cave. It was a wonderful, rich, scary scene, and even Sylvie, who lived through the story dozens of times a day, felt a shiver on meeting the dreadful old man.

The creature led her up some stairs to a different room, one filled with a great roaring sound. Sylvie realised that a cascade of water formed one whole wall of the chamber. They were behind the waterfall!

He would help her in her quest, he shouted over the pounding water, but she would have to do him a favour first. His fierce eyes glared, his white beard waggled and the gash on his forehead seemed to pulse as he spoke.

At first she wasn't sure she had heard him correctly. "Heal you?" she shouted back. "How can I heal you?"

He pointed at the wound. "Only the pure kiss of a princess can heal it!"

Princess Sylvie, who had the ability to enter into her part completely, recoiled in horror, as always. But on this particular day, she noticed something she hadn't before: the glitter of a tear in the corner of the old man's eye. No Reader would have noticed it, with so much else to take in, but Sylvie was shocked. Here was a character no one liked. His appearance was horrid and his voice so deathly awful that even Prince Riggeloff, who was afraid of no one, steered clear of him. It was a voice that seemed to come from a coffin at the bottom of a mine shaft. And yet here he was with a tear in his eye. Was it possible that even the Keeper of the Cave was feeling the same stress that afflicted everyone else?

Sylvie waited till the end of the story, after the spell had been broken and the Keeper of the Cave turned into mild young Prince Godric – the extremely handsome person with whom Sylvie was supposed to live happily ever after. The book closed gently, and the back-up lights blinked on.

"You seemed upset," she told Godric in her quick soft voice. Sylvie had a confiding way of talking that put other characters at ease. Somehow it didn't work with Godric.

"B-beg pardon, Princess?" Godric said, turning his gold crown in his hand.

"Back in Chapter Three. There were tears in your eyes."

"There were?"

"Before you changed. When you were storming around in the Cave of Diamonds?"

"Oh, *him*. I truh-try not to think about him."

"But aren't you the same person?"

"I hope not!"

"But you have to be. He turns *into* you."

Prince Godric didn't answer. He just continued to fiddle with his crown. The sunlight glanced off it, throwing gleams of light in all directions. "You wouldn't understand," he said at last. "You're always the s-same."

"What wouldn't I understand?"

"How hard it is being two people."

"Why is it hard?" she asked. "I'm a thousand people, now that our book's in print again."

"No," he replied. "You're the same puh-person a thousand times."

She looked at him. A pleasant enough fellow, though he always stuttered when he spoke to her. Why was that? No one else had trouble talking to her. The truth was, she didn't care for Godric very much, blindingly handsome though he was. If his other self was repulsive, his princely self was weak.

"I have to be *two* people a thousand times," he said. "I meet him around every cuh-corner!" He glanced at her to see if she was still listening.

Sylvie folded her arms. "You don't like the Keeper of the Cave very much."

Godric looked at her, then down at his crown, which he continued to turn in his hands. He seemed hypnotised by the beams of light it threw off.

"Not that I blame you," Sylvie continued. "He scares me every time I do a scene with him."

Godric mumbled something.

"What?"

He looked up. "He scares me too."

Sylvie shook her head. "Godric," she said, "Godric, Godric."

A large green bird with yellow breast feathers lifted

into the air, crying, "*Raawwk!* Reader! Reader!"

"Well!" Sylvie gave Godric a quick smile. "That's our cue."

He turned away. "Don't watch."

"For heaven's sake, Godric, I've seen you change thousands of times."

"I hate this part!"

Before her eyes, his noble nose began to crumple slightly and his clear brow grew furrows. His wavy hair turned grey; his skull grew bulbous. Godric – no longer Godric – seemed to grow larger and smaller at the same time. His shoulders stooped over, but swelled with twisted musculature. His eyes turned bleary, but fierce.

"I told you not to watch!" he snarled. His voice had deepened a whole octave and seemed to come from somewhere beneath his feet. "Now GET OUT!"

Chapter Three

The brass sundial in the courtyard could tell you what time of day it was, but not the week, month, or year. And since the weather was different in every chapter, you couldn't even be sure of the season. But finally a day came, accompanied by a chill breeze and a sky like tarnished silver, when the drawbridge lowered to let three creaking wagons cross, mounded high with the new costumes. The king made a proclamation about it, which was greeted, as always, with applause and trumpets, and before long the courtyard was crowded with characters from as far away as Part Three, all anxious to see their new clothes. Oohing and ahhing, the ladies-in-waiting examined the golden ribbons festooning their slimmer gowns. Queen Emmeline, who seldom showed pleasure, actually blushed when her maidservant brought her a long red velvet dress trimmed at the collar and cuffs with ivory lace. Sylvie was a slim girl who hadn't gained or lost a penny's weight since 1917, but she was given several outfits as well. None of them was the sort that she could climb trees in (medieval princesses were not issued "play clothes"); but she had fewer flounces and ruffles to deal with, thank goodness. Sylvie especially liked the dark green riding cloak with its narrow border of light green; it would be perfect for her adventures in the forest. There were also three pairs of identical blue leather shoes, to replace the ones she had ruined.

But there was still no sign of Sylvie's friend, the young person known simply as the girl with dark blue eyes. Like Norbert Fangl, the girl had had a long life as an actual person in the outer world, yet she appeared no older than the princess. Instinctively, Sylvie's hand went to her locket, rubbing it gently. She clicked it open. There was her friend peering out at her, her small mouth pursed as if determined to be serious. Would she be getting a new costume, too? She seemed to need nothing, and her comings and goings had little to do with the plot. Being a minor character (an assistant to the third lady-in-waiting) gave the girl that freedom, especially since she had no lines to say; but still it seemed almost *illegal* for her to disappear for days at a time.

Near midnight, under the usual full moon, the princess wandered alone by the Mere. The wind was blowing the water into waves, and she was glad she had the new green cloak, so much warmer than the old one. Just then, a movement in the water caught her eye. It wasn't a wave, but a swirling motion, as if something large and powerful were beneath the surface.

"Fish," Sylvie breathed. "Is it you, Fish?"

The circular movements came closer to the shore; then an enormous dorsal fin lifted slowly from the water.

"It *is* you!" Sylvie jumped up and down, ignoring the fact that her new shoes were getting soaked.

She loved her invisible fish, who always saved her by gulping her down and carrying her to the bottom of the Mere where the thieves could not find her. The beast was large as a cavern and transparent as a crystal punch bowl. Suddenly, it heaved the top half of its body above the surface, and Sylvie peered in to see if it were carrying any passengers. That's where she sometimes discovered her friend with the dark blue eyes returning from one of her mysterious journeys. The fish was empty this time. It swam in slow circles by the shore, like a cat rubbing against a trouser leg; then it sank out of sight.

"Hi," came a voice behind her.

Sylvie whirled around. There, on a hillock of dune grass, stood a young girl in a blue cape, her long brown hair lifting from her shoulders. Her mouth was unsmiling, but her eyes were bright.

"You!" Sylvie shouted. They both laughed.

"I don't *always* arrive by fish," said the girl with the dark blue eyes as the friends started walking along the shore.

"How did you know I was looking for you?"

"I know the way your mind works."

"Not everybody around here does."

"That's right." The girl gave Sylvie a knowing look. "Are we talking about Prince Godric?" she said.

"There you go, reading my mind again," Sylvie said.

"What about him?"

"He seems to think he's in love with me."

"Of course he is."

"I'm not in love with him."

"Of course you're not."

Sylvie had to smile. "You have a way of making things sound so simple."

"They are. He's a man of feeling. You're a girl of action. It's not that you don't feel things. It's just that —" the girl made a long flowing motion with her arms — "you don't *feeeel* things."

Sylvie laughed until she hiccuped. "It's true!"

"You love helpless creatures. He loves helpless maidens. As he calls them."

Sylvie nodded. "Still," she said.

Her friend, who'd been looking at the lights in the distant castle, turned back to the princess. "Still?"

Sylvie gave a little sigh. "Still, he's got a real problem."

"Oh, I know. It's hard being anyone. Being two people is — it's almost unfair."

"Yes," said Sylvie earnestly. "And two such different people."

"But I can't do anything about that," said the girl crisply. "He needs to have two personalities for the story. The story has to come first."

There was something tremendously refreshing about the girl with the dark blue eyes. You never knew what

33

she'd say, but it was always something simple and true. It could also seem a little heartless.

"*Why* does the story have to come first?" Sylvie said.

"That's not a question a fictional character should have to ask."

"But Godric's got more stress than anyone."

The girl looked curiously at Princess Sylvie. "Where did you ever hear that word? It's nowhere in the book."

"The Writer told it to me."

"The Writer."

"Lily. She says she has stress, too, and she'd like to write in a character who can help us with ours."

The girl with the dark blue eyes was silent. "What sort of character?" she said at last.

"I don't know. Someone she knows. A friend, she said."

"A real person, then."

"I think so."

"I wonder where she got that idea."

Sylvie blushed. "I'm afraid I may have had something to do with it."

"Really!"

Sylvie was again reminded that her friend was

different from other characters. Not only had she been a real person, but she had to be older than the story itself, because she'd once told Sylvie that she was the book's first Reader. It was hard to see that in the twelve-year-old girl she appeared to be.

"I admit," the girl said, "we've never had a problem like this before."

"Like what?"

"More Readers than we know what to do with. But that can't last for long. Books don't *stay* popular. Can't everyone just be patient?"

"Patient? Have you met my mother?" Sylvie said with a smile.

The girl didn't answer. She wasn't really listening. Sometimes she seemed so far away she might be in a different world.

"What are you thinking about?" Sylvie said suddenly.

"Just now? Somebody you don't know."

"I like knowing things I don't know."

"That's right, you do. Well, do you remember Ricky?"

"Who could forget Ricky? He burned the book."

"That was decades ago. Well, Ricky had a son, and

his son had a son. All named Ricky. I was thinking about the grandson."

"Really? Why?"

"Because he worries me."

"Ricky's grandson?" Sylvie was puzzled. "I'm not good at keeping track of time, but didn't you die before he was born?"

"Many years before he was born."

"Then how do you even know about him?"

"I watch after the family. Watch *over* them, you might say."

"Even into the future?"

"Especially into the future."

"And what's wrong with little Ricky?"

The girl smiled. "Nothing's wrong with him, except he's just like his grandfather."

"Oh my."

"Yes."

"Is that why you disappear from the book for days at a time?"

"Well, it's one reason."

Sylvie shook her head wonderingly. "There's so much I don't know about you."

Her friend smiled, now completely back from

wherever her mind had taken her. "You're not supposed to know about me. I'm supposed to know about you."

"I don't even know your name."

The girl looked at Sylvie. "That's true."

"I can't believe I don't know your name!" Sylvie said, realising the fact fully. "You were always just 'the girl with the dark blue eyes'."

"Call me –" The girl paused. "Well, what name comes to mind when you think of me?"

"I don't know."

"Try."

Sylvie thought, but it was no use. "All I can think of is that dream."

"Which one? There have been so many."

"When you were dying."

"I was doing a lot of dreaming back then."

"Not you. Your granddaughter. You were dying and Claire had a dream about you, that you were a young girl hiding in the laurel bushes."

"Yes, that was a good dream."

"You were hiding in the laurel bushes, looking just as young as you are now. I always connect you with that."

"Well, it's funny," the girl said. "That happens to be my name."

"Bush?"

"No, Laurel."

Sylvie let the sound of it roll over her tongue. "I like it."

The girl laughed. It was good to see her in bright spirits again. Sylvie decided not to mention anything more about the plan to write in a new character. If Laurel (what a nice name!) didn't like the idea, they would just call the whole thing off!

The scene was not going well. The queen had called the footman a dunderhead — a word that appears nowhere in her dialogue — because he had brought her the hard green pillow rather than the soft blue one for her throne. It was alarming to hear Queen Emmeline veering from the text like this.

Sylvie was saying, "I'm sorry. I can't marry anyone."

"What do you *MEAN?*" her mother barked, and everyone jumped. She looked around, then cleared her throat and tried again. (That's another thing she never did. Once a line is delivered, you're not supposed to go back.) "What do you mean, dear?"

"I have everything," Sylvie replied, continuing her dialogue from the book, "but I have done nothing. Before I marry, I must do one Great Good Thing."

Just then she heard whispering outside the throne room – a woman's voice saying, "Who's that?"

A man's voice shushed her. "That's Princess Sylvie."

"I like her."

"Shh! Of course you like her; she's the heroine."

"Don't you think marrying Prince Riggeloff is doing a great thing?" The king was talking louder than usual to drown out the whispering.

"Who's he?"

"Shh. Who do you think?"

Sylvie glanced at the entranceway, but saw no one. "No," she said, picking up the dialogue. "Even if I trusted him, which I don't –"

"But this is absurd!" exclaimed the queen hotly. As she turned around, the sleeve of her robe caught on a pewter goblet and swept it off the side table. It clattered to the floor, splattering wine everywhere.

Sylvie looked at her a moment, then repeated: "Even if I trusted him –"

"Who left that prop on that table?" shouted the queen.

"Even if I trusted him," the princess soldiered on, "which I don't –"

"Get the servants in here! Who is responsible?"

In the brief silence that followed, the whispering voice could be heard clearly. "Is she always like this?"

"It's been getting worse," a man's voice whispered back.

"I'm *waiting,*" warned the queen with her arms crossed.

"Which I don't –"

"I can't *stand* this!" The queen had tears in her angry eyes.

The Chief Councillor came up and put a reassuring arm around her shoulder. He tried to lead her away.

"Which I don't," Princess Sylvie somehow continued, though her lower lip was trembling. "Marrying is what I do *after* I do the Great Good Thing."

"What a mess!" came a different voice, nasal and echoing, from somewhere overhead. There was no roof on the castle and the face of an enormous boy was looking down. "Who can read this stuff?"

Suddenly the book slammed shut. Everything went dark. For a few seconds Sylvie heard nothing except the sound of sobbing. "Mother, it's all right," she said into the darkness.

There was a buzz and a brief flicker, and then the back-up lights came on. The Reader was gone. To everyone's astonishment, a tall young woman hurried into the throne room.

"Hey, get back here!" called a guard, poking his head in.

"Excuse me, Your Majesty," said the woman, bowing her head.

The queen fixed her with an outraged eye. "Who sent for a shepherdess?"

The pretty stranger was carrying a shepherd's crook and wearing a scooped peasant blouse tied with a string. She also wore a flowered skirt and soft, mouse-coloured shoes; but what struck Sylvie most was her long chestnut hair. Instead of draping over her shoulders, the hair moved in slow waves behind her, although there was not a breath of breeze in the castle.

"Never mind me," said the woman. "Just breathe. You're not breathing."

"Of course I'm breathing!" the queen retorted. "What do you think I'm doing?"

"Slowly. Breathe slowly. Just do as I say."

"I don't do as anyone says. Get this person out of here!" But something in the young woman's voice caught her attention. "What's wrong with my breathing?"

"Do it for me." The woman's voice was a liquid alto. "Breathe slowly. That's it. Deeper. Don't breathe up in your chest. Breathe down into your belly."

"'Belly' is an indecent word." But Queen Emmeline did as she was told.

"Now exhale *slowly*. Slower. That's it. Beautiful!"

There was no question, the queen was growing calmer.

"Three more now," said the young woman. "Sip slowly down into your centre. That's it. Slower-slower-slower. Good. Now exhale and let the breath rise like a fountain."

The queen eyed the stranger suspiciously, but obeyed. After two breaths, she'd had enough. "All right, now who *are* you?"

"I think I know!" said Sylvie with a sudden smile. "Aren't you a friend of Lily's?"

The woman turned her remarkable eyes on the princess. "Do you know Lily?"

"Mother, this is the person the Writer was going to put into the story!"

The queen looked at the stranger as if appraising a piece of jewellery. "Well, well."

"What is your name, dear?" said King Walther.

"Rosetta."

"Just Rosetta?"

"Stein," she said. "Rosetta Stein. I'm a yoga instructor."

The king and queen looked at each other in puzzlement.

"It's an ancient discipline from the Far East. You really haven't heard of yoga?"

"All we have in the east, my dear," said King Walther, "is a considerable forest."

"Still," the queen said, "you were sent here to help us with our distress."

"I think you mean 'stress,' Mother," said Sylvie.

"Oh, yoga is very good for stress. But I don't understand. I was *sent* here?"

"Lily wrote you in!" said Sylvie triumphantly.

"Wrote me into what?"

"Our book! *The Great Good Thing*."

"What!" Rosetta's hair flicked about in the air behind her like a nervous animal.

A skinny fellow in a black doublet stepped forwards. "Perhaps I can explain," he said, with a smile. "My name is Norbert Fangl. Like you, I was a real person in the outside world. Not many of us here can say that."

"Glad to meet you," said Rosetta, shaking his hand.

"Thank you. When I died some years ago . . ."

Rosetta pulled her hand away. "You're a dead person?"

"Not at all. I'm a memory. People's memory of Norbert Fangl."

"That's right," said Princess Sylvie with pride. "But he was being forgotten, so I got him written into the story!"

"A generous act for which I will be forever grateful, Princess."

"Are you saying I'm dead?" Rosetta said.

"No, no," said Fangl.

"Because I'm not."

"That's what's so interesting," he continued. "In the outer world, you are Miss Stein, a living person. But here you are the Writer's *version* of Miss Stein."

"I'm myself!" said Rosetta with conviction.

"Of course you are. But which version? Your own, or Lily's?"

"Now *this,*" piped up Pingree the Jester, "is interesting!" He jumped onto the table and pranced about delightedly. "Where's Godric? Get this lady together with Prince Godric! He's two people, too. What a couple they'd make!"

"Pingree," said Sylvie.

"Come to think, they'd make a *couple* of couples!"

"Pingree!"

He cocked an eyebrow. "Yes, Princess?"

"Be quiet."

"Can you really teach us this so-called discipline of yours?" said the queen.

"If you're willing."

"I'll try just about anything!"

With that, the king and queen, along with Sylvie and Norbert Fangl, escorted the surprising shepherdess into the council room to talk over her duties.

Chapter Four

*I*t was a fine morning, and Sylvie found Fangl out
on the east turret going through his papers. Sun glint-
ed off his bald spot, and a light breeze riffled the pages
of scribbles and geometric figures that he'd gathered
about him on the bench. Below, the castle's huge shadow gave a blue tinge to the lilies in the moat. Beyond
that, in buttery sunlight, the road led through a pine
grove towards Humped Mountain and the distant
Mere of Remind.

"You weren't in class this morning," Sylvie said.

No response.

"Fangl?"

He looked up. "Oh, hello, Princess."

"You weren't in class."

"Ah, Miss Stein's yoga instruction. I'm afraid I couldn't get there today."

"You missed yesterday, too."

He nodded. "I meant to go. I find her class very helpful in clarifying my mind."

"But?"

Just then, the wind picked up a piece of paper and sailed it towards the parapet.

"Get it! Quick!" cried Fangl, struggling to his feet and spilling a sheaf of papers on the floor.

Sylvie jumped up the wall and caught the flying page just in time.

"Thank you!" said Fangl, taking it gratefully. "That was two day's work!"

Sylvie frowned at the shape her tutor had drawn. "It looks like a spider's web."

"That's perceptive of you, dear. I've learned a great deal from observing the arachnids."

"A rack?"

"Spiders. They are masters of geometry. Once you enter their web, there is no escape."

Webs. Why did that sound familiar? She turned her head sideways for a better look at the drawing. "So what is this you're working on?"

Fangl's grey eyebrows rose and his eyes grew almost mischievous.

"Is it a secret?" she pursued.

"If I were alive," he said, "it would be the greatest secret in the world."

"What *is* it?"

"Well," he said, looking out briefly over the parapet, as if to see if someone were listening, "you remember the shapes I've been teaching you. Cubes, rhomboids, tetrahedrons?"

She nodded vigorously.

"All fine, useful shapes. Couldn't do without them. But I've always felt there was something else, some shape no one had yet discovered."

"And you've discovered it?"

"I believe I'm close. I'm very close."

"What's it like?"

"Hard to describe. It's a shape that implies the others. I think of it as the perfect shape."

"Not a hexagon," mused Sylvie, looking at the page. "Not an octagon."

"It's not like any other polygon. I call it," said Fangl, and paused just a moment, "I call it the Paragon."

Sylvie's eyes widened. "It sounds wonderful!" The

truth was, she didn't know why her dear old tutor was so excited about a drawing, but it was delightful to see the glow of pleasure on his face. Fangl was always kind, always pleasant, but Sylvie hadn't noticed that he was particularly happy, until now.

"And nobody knows about this?"

He lowered his voice, although there was no one nearby and his words were scattered by the breeze. "I've only told you," he said, "because you saved my life, by getting me into this story."

"Thank you, Fangl."

Norbert Fangl shook his head in wonder. "Who would have thought I'd accomplish my greatest work after I died?"

"Excuse me for asking, but is there some actual *use* for this shape?"

"I would think a shape this wonderful would have many important uses. I just don't know what they are."

"Of course." Sylvie smiled. "I'm happy for you, Fangl," she said, giving his skinny shoulder a squeeze.

Later that day, Sylvie was struggling through the book's climactic scene, in which the wretched Keeper of the Cave appears behind the waterfall to make his terrible demand for the third and final time. By now, the wound on his forehead has become such an agony that he falls to the ground unconscious. It is at this moment that the princess finally takes pity on him. The simple words she has to say never fail to move her: "Sleep, sleep, old man."

Then she bends towards him to kiss his wound, breaking the spell he has lived under for years.

This time, however, as Princess Sylvie was about to say her lines, she glanced through the veil of roaring water and saw several sheep grazing on a nearby hillside. A shepherdess was looking over in her direction. Rosetta Stein. Since Rosetta was a background character with no lines to say, it was natural for her to watch the story from the side. But still, seeing her threw Sylvie off, and instead of saying, "Sleep, sleep, old man," as she'd intended, she murmured, "Sheep, sheep, old man," before she caught herself, appalled.

To the Reader (a twelve-year-old boy with dark-framed glasses), the mistake appeared as a typographical error, and he took off his glasses and rubbed his eyes. When he looked again, the correct words were in place, and Sylvie went on. But she felt shaken. It didn't help matters that during a break between Readers, Pingree the Jester came by and made a loud bleating sound, to the amusement of Riggeloff and his pack of ruffians.

Sylvie was still a little off balance the next morning during Rosetta's yoga class. She enjoyed these classes, which were held in a garden in the inner courtyard. Since Sylvie was an authentic character who always meant what she said, Rosetta's instruction to move from the core outward made sense. In most ways, she was already centred. But she wasn't feeling centred today.

Every character with a speaking part had been required, by royal decree, to attend the class at least once, so during the first week the sessions had been crowded; but they'd thinned out after that. Pingree was the first to drop. He thrived on commotion, not calmness, and his humour depended on keeping people *off* balance, not *in* balance.

Prince Riggeloff was the next to quit, along with most of his retainers. When Rosetta asked why, he answered, civilly enough, that he was an angry character, and that if he became calm he would not be able to do his job. The truth was, he *liked* being angry, taking revenge, stealing treasure, plotting crimes.

Those who remained began the class by lying down on

blankets or small rugs – except the queen, who had a special mattress brought for her. Mattress or not, Queen Emmeline had trouble getting into the spirit of things.

"Now lie down in Corpse Pose and close your eyes," Rosetta intoned in her resonant voice, her hair floating behind her. "We're going to breathe deeply, not into the chest, but into the cave in the belly."

"I love this part," Prince Godric whispered to Sylvie.

"Really?"

"I *live* in a cave. I can almost feel the diamonds glittering inside me."

Sylvie giggled.

"What?" he whispered.

"Wouldn't that give you a tummy ache?"

"We carry the cave within us," Rosetta continued. "Everyone has this same centre. It is the seat of power."

"Yes, yes," said the queen, her eyes snapping open. "But can't we hurry up? We might have a Reader at any moment."

Rosetta smiled. "Hurry up and relax?"

"And this lying down business. I don't like lying down in front of people."

"They all have their eyes closed."

"They're peeking."

Sylvie giggled again. "Sorry," she said, but couldn't stop herself. Everything seemed funny today, even Rosetta's hair, which sailed out behind her without any breeze at all.

"How does she *do* that?" Sylvie asked her friend Laurel that night as they walked beside the Mere.

"That's the way Lily described her. I think it's a nice touch. It makes me think Lily actually has some writing talent."

"But Readers aren't supposed to notice Rosetta, are they? She doesn't even have any lines."

"True, she's a background character. But she adds colour to the story, don't you think?"

Sylvie seemed unconvinced.

"You know," said Laurel, "even a small change can have a big effect. When you drop a pebble in a pool, the ripples go out all the way to the edge and back to the centre again. Every drop of water is affected."

Sylvie was silent.

"It doesn't matter how plain or insignificant the stone."

Sylvie nodded.

"And as stones go, Miss Stein is neither plain nor insignificant."

"No, she isn't."

"Quite the opposite."

Sylvie picked up a smooth piece of quartz and hurled it far out into the Mere. "She's always watching when I'm trying to do my scenes."

"What's wrong with that?"

"It throws me off."

The water lapped softly as they continued along.

"Remember," said Laurel, "you asked to have her come."

"I didn't ask for *her*. I just wanted someone to give Mother an occasional shoulder rub."

"You got more than you bargained for. We always do."

"If Lily could put her in, she can take her *out*," Sylvie declared.

Her friend didn't answer. She was quiet so long, in fact, that Sylvie finally asked if something was wrong.

"I don't like the way you think of this story," Laurel said slowly. "As if it were yours to change when you don't like something."

"I didn't mean —"

"Remember, it's not even Lily's story. She just wrote it down so it could be published again."

"So whose is it?"

The girl turned her dark blue eyes on Princess Sylvie. "Don't you know?"

As Sylvie returned her gaze, she had the oddest feeling, as if she were looking into a tunnel that led out into a dark blue sky. It made her dizzy.

"No, I don't," she said, looking away. She wished suddenly that she could end this conversation.

A few moments later, a garish bird flashed by overhead crying, "Reader! Reader!" and Sylvie hurried off, relieved for an excuse to get away from her dearest friend in the world.

Chapter Five

"My jewels!" screamed the queen. "They've been stolen!"

"Sleep, sleep, old man."

"After her, fools!" snarled Riggeloff.

The book seemed to be getting more popular by the week, and the pace of life more hectic. Laurel had assured the princess it couldn't last, but in the meantime there were so many faces peering down from the sky that Sylvie barely noticed them any more. She was too busy finding her place, saying her lines and hurrying on. Sometimes she or another character didn't arrive in time, and the Reader would look puzzled. The truth is, no one reads a story; one *overhears* it; and if the characters aren't there, living and suffering on the page before you, nothing makes sense. At such moments (luckily they were few), Readers assumed that their minds had been wandering. Then the characters would stagger in, and the story continued.

Rosetta, after having little to do at first, soon found herself as busy as most of the others. Besides her morning yoga class, she gave private lessons when she wasn't needed to cross the page with her sheep behind the main characters. She worked especially with the more highly-strung courtiers on stress-reducing exercises in an ante-chamber of the castle, out of the Reader's line of sight.

Once, even Prince Riggeloff summoned her. She had had few dealings with him before and wasn't prepared for his way of talking. "Neck rub, wench," he barked, flopping down on his stomach.

When Miss Stein didn't respond, he grew nasty. She turned and walked out of the room.

"Come back, wench!"

"Shh," whispered the king's Chief Councillor. "The Reader can hear you all the way from page 69!"

"Blast the Reader!"

Rosetta stood outside on the sunny path and closed her eyes, calming herself, then went to find Sylvie, who just then was freeing the blind owl from the thorn bush. The wounded bird was struggling, about to burst into the air, when a distant voice called to the Reader, who seemed to be in a school of some kind: "Tanesha, can you tell us the names of the planets?" The book shut quickly.

"Ouch!" cried Sylvie. "The owl scratched me!" When the back-up lights came on, Sylvie was frowning and sucking her hand. "Oh, hi, Rose," she said.

"Are you all right?"

"I wish Readers wouldn't shut the book so fast. It scares the animals."

A servant hurried over with a bandage, but the princess waved him off irritably. "How would that look to the next Reader? Think about it!"

"You are so good at what you do!" Rosetta said.

"I know." Sylvie looked at her hand critically. It seemed to have stopped bleeding. "You are too."

"Not everyone seems to think so. I just came from the prince."

"Yes?"

"I didn't care for the way he spoke to me."

"I can't believe Prince Godric would speak to you disrespectfully."

"No," Rosetta said, "the other prince."

"Oh!" Sylvie smiled. "You have to remember, Riggeloff's just behaving the way his character is written."

"He was insulting."

"He's got nobility in him, too, but he can be very bad. He *has* to be bad."

"I keep forgetting," said Rosetta recklessly, "I'm not out in the real world where people have free will."

"Oh?" Sylvie was starting to feel a little insulted herself. "What do you mean, 'the real world'?"

"You know. Flesh and blood. Actual life."

"I have actual life." She blew on her hand and gave it a shake. "You know, Readers come and go. They get old and they disappear. I live forever. You tell me who is more real."

Rosetta nodded and puffed out a sigh. "I guess I'm just upset about Riggeloff."

"Was he very terrible?"

"He called me a wench, which I actually thought was cute. But it was his tone. He treated me as if I were nothing more than a slave."

Sylvie looked at her in surprise. "You're not a slave, but you *are* a servant."

"I beg your pardon."

"He should not have been disrespectful. But you are a servant – a servant disguised as a shepherdess. Surely you knew that?"

Rosetta stared at her. She seemed about to say many things, but held back. Finally she said, "Maybe I'd better go home."

"What do you mean?"

"Home. Back to Croton Falls where I came from."

Sylvie shook her head. "I don't think you can."

"What did you say?"

"You're part of the book now."

"You mean I'm a *prisoner* as well as a slave?"

"You're not a sl–"

But Rosetta wasn't listening. Without a word she turned and walked out of the chapter.

Next morning, Rosetta did not show up to teach her yoga class. Young Prince Godric looked bewildered. He and the others had been making progress on a new exercise Miss Stein was teaching them: projecting energy from the centre of their bodies. They hadn't succeeded completely, but now and then one glimpsed a thin blue line of electricity lasting a second or two before it fizzled out. Godric was hoping to develop this power as protection against his frightening other self.

He had gained more confidence since taking Rosetta's class and had almost stopped stuttering. Sylvie felt guilty as she watched him trudge back towards Humped Mountain.

"But she *is* a servant," she whispered under her breath. "Isn't she?"

Queen Emmeline called out from a narrow window slit in the castle keep. "Where is that shepherdess friend of yours? Send her in at once!"

"I'll look for her!" Sylvie called back. Privately, she winced at her mother's tone. What would Rose have felt about it? Suddenly it seemed urgent to find her. Sylvie hurried across the drawbridge, but before she reached the pine grove, a Reader interrupted. He was an elderly man with a disconcerting way of reading certain sentences over again slowly, to savour them, so of course the characters had to play those scenes again, sometimes in slow motion. It was very hard, they found, to do a chase scene in slow motion. Also, the old man kept moving back and forth, forth and back, probably on a rocking chair, and several of the characters began to feel queasy. It was taking forever to get through Part One.

At last, he slipped a tasselled strip of leather between

the pages, and Sylvie raced off towards the shep-herdess's hut without even waiting for the back-up lights to come on. In those few pitch-dark seconds, she ran smack into Thomas, the thief who had always admired Sylvie.

"Oh!" she cried, as the lights flittered on. She had knocked Thomas on his back and fallen on top of him. "Are you all right?"

"I think so," he said, touching his forehead gingerly. Long-stemmed irises were scattered around him where he'd dropped them. His hair had been brushed carefully to one side. "Have you seen Miss Stein?"

"I'm looking for her myself." She stared at his hair and then at the flowers. "Well," she said lightly, "nice bumping into you." What was *that* about? she thought, hurrying up the lane past a flutter of white ducks.

Miss Stein's cottage was a small, muffin-shaped hut with a thatched roof and a dirt path leading up to a sin-gle stone step and an unpainted door. Sylvie knocked. She heard the scrape of a chair, and then a creak as the door opened and the tall, dark-eyed young woman stood before her. For a long moment, neither said a word. "I'm sorry," Sylvie said at last.

Rosetta tilted her head. "Why?"

Sylvie took a deep breath. "Because I said a hurtful thing."

Rosetta nodded. "Do you want to come in?"

"Yes, thanks." Sylvie entered a low, dark room whose only light came through a small window at the far end. She had never been inside a shepherdess's hut before. From a distance, the cottages looked charming. Inside, they were cramped and dreary, with stale air and floors of hard-packed dirt. Still, she could see that Rosetta had added nice touches, jars filled with flowers, bright curtains and even a drawing of some kind on the ceiling over the bed.

"Have a seat," Rosetta said, showing her the one chair. "I was just making tea." She took the puffing kettle off the fire and poured mint tea for both of them.

Sylvie watched the leaves settle in the clay mug. "Look, I don't know how much time we have before another Reader comes along, but I didn't like our last conversation."

"I hated it."

Sylvie leaned forwards on her elbows. "Rose, someone should have explained things to you when you first got here. You aren't a prisoner. It's just that every character has a purpose."

"And mine is?"

"To serve those who need you."

Rosetta nodded. "Well, you're honest. Listen, I *like* to be of service. Prince Godric, for instance. He's a dear man and I love helping him get some power over his situation. When you think of what he's up against . . .!"

"I know he loves your classes."

"And he's making progress. Energy projection is not easy. It's just . . ."

"What?"

"Well, I can't be ordered around."

"Nobody likes being ordered around."

"No, I mean I *can't* be. You could say my character wasn't written that way. My talent is centring myself and then acting from that centre. It's what I do. It's what I can help other people do. When people give me orders, I just close down. That's how I felt with Prince Riggeloff."

"He can be difficult."

"How do you *deal* with him?"

Sylvie shrugged. "I deal with him the way a heroine deals with a villain."

Rose shook her head. "I wish I could be that brave."

Sylvie was glad the room was dim, because she was blushing. "I'm sure you're very brave."

"Not like you."

"Well, you're good at other things. Look at the way you've decorated this place."

"Thanks."

"Although I probably wouldn't draw pictures of spiders' webs over my bed."

Rosetta followed her eyes. "They aren't spiders' webs, they're constellations."

"What's that?"

"Stars. Don't you know about stars?"

"Yes!" cried Sylvie, standing on tiptoe for a closer look. "I remember now. I used to see them from the window at night, years and years ago. That's when we weren't living inside a book."

"You weren't *what*?"

"It sounds strange, I know, but some boy set our book on fire – accidentally, we think – and for years we managed to live in his sister's memory. That's when I found out about stars. The sky was filled with them. We haven't had any since the book was republished."

"You will, when the moon isn't so full."

"The moon is always full."

"Out in the real — I mean, the *other* world," Rosetta said, "the moon gets bigger and smaller and sometimes doesn't come out at all. That's when you see the stars best."

"Do they really have all those lines between them? I don't remember that."

Rosetta looked up at her drawing of the constellations of Ursa Major, Ursa Minor, and Cassiopeia, with the North Star in the middle. "No, I drew the lines to connect them, so you can see the pattern."

"I thought at first it was that web that Lily was talking about."

Rosetta looked puzzled.

"She told me," said Sylvie, "that she was going to put our book into a web."

"Ah!" Rosetta laughed. "I see!" She tried to explain to Sylvie what a computer was, and then what the Internet was. "Lily told me her story was going to be uploaded on the Web, but I didn't think much about it."

"I haven't told the others," said Sylvie. "I didn't want to scare them."

"What's scary about cyberspace?"

"To be ripped out of their book and thrown into a web?"

"It's just electronic connections. If I can understand it, anybody can." She could see Sylvie didn't. "Don't worry; you'll know soon enough. I think it's supposed to happen on the morning of the twenty-fifth." She looked at Sylvie in surprise. "Isn't that tomorrow?"

"I have no idea."

"Maybe you should tell the king."

"You're right!" And with no more than a quick goodbye, Sylvie ran from the cottage.

"Princess! What does it say? What does it *say?*" The big woman gestured at the proclamation. It was one of several posted within the outer walls of the castle.

Sylvie dodged a ragged boy who was chasing a chicken among the vegetable stalls. "Oh dear. It says we must all pack our belongings *immediately,*" said Sylvie, squinting at the document. "We're moving out."

"That's what the blacksmith said, but I didn't believe 'im. How do I pack up all *this?*" She pointed a thick finger to her table mounded high with fish.

"I don't know," Sylvie said, turning away from the strong smell. She needed to talk to her father. "Maybe you won't have to. Don't do anything until I get back."

Princess Sylvie raced through the rutted marketplace, her ribbons flying. How could her father have misunderstood her? When she spoke to him, she had meant to reassure him, not send everyone into a panic. Sylvie had no clear idea what it meant to be "uploaded", but was sure it had nothing to do with loading fish onto wagons.

In the great hall, she passed a servant hurrying past with a stack of bed linen. Two workmen were taking down a tapestry.

"Where's my father?"

One of the men pointed towards the stone staircase. "In the treasury, I think."

Sylvie took the stairs three at a time, almost knocking down a porter struggling with a trunk. Her father was not in the treasury, nor in the council chamber. She pelted up the spiral stairs to the round room at the top of the tower, only to find it empty. Breathing hard, she leaned against the wall. Where *was* he? She slid onto a narrow chair to catch her breath. A looking glass stood opposite, and she noticed that her hair was coming undone. That was always happening – maybe because she was always running. Her face was flushed, and a long twirl of fine brown hair was hanging right down over her nose.

As she was poking it in place, she noticed a ladder leading through a narrow hole to the very top of the keep and scrambled up. Sure enough, there stood King Walther, dressed to the throat in regal purple, looking over the parapet.

"Father," she said. The wind immediately made a mess of her hair. His was held firmly by his ermine-trimmed crown.

He didn't turn, but stared out at the distant buildings, woods, Mere, and mountain. "A beautiful illustration," he said at last. "Don't you think?"

"Very beautiful, Father."

"Why would anyone want to destroy such a picture?"

"Father, listen. Nobody's going to destroy our kingdom. Lily wouldn't do that."

He turned finally and shook his head. "I know you say that, but you remember as well as I do the time when we had to leave the book and go to another land. We almost didn't survive."

Sylvie couldn't argue. Even now it gave her a pang to think how close they had come to extinction. "I think it's different this time," she said. "Rose explained to me about these computer things."

"I admire Miss Stein, but we have our own scientists. They've looked into the matter and inform me that a computer is a form of abacus, a counting device. Counting won't help us now."

"Maybe she means something different. She says it has to do with electricity."

"What are you talking about?"

"Haven't you heard of electricity?"

"Of course. What is it?"

"Well," Sylvie began uncertainly, "I think it's the same thing that lightning is made of."

"Lightning! So once again we're to be burned up!"

Sylvie shook her head helplessly. "Rosetta explained it better."

"Your Majesty?"

They whirled around to see Sylvie's friend Laurel climbing out onto the parapet. "Ah," the king said. "How did you find us?"

Laurel straightened the shoulder of her blue cape and gave a curtsy. "I was down in the market, and I looked up."

"You always come in times of trouble," the king said, "and you're always a comfort. But there's nothing you can do this time."

"True, I don't know much about computers; but I don't think you need fear them. Didn't Lily use one to write this book?"

"But now we're being taken out of the book and put – I can't stand to think about it!"

"We need to trust Lily more," said Laurel quietly. "She's a good girl."

"But still, some great change is going to happen, isn't that true?"

"Apparently so."

"And it's to happen tomorrow morning?"

"That's what she said."

"The farmer will be at his plough," murmured the king. "The queen will be having her muffin."

Sylvie went to him and put an arm around his waist. "Father, I think we should do what we always do when great things are happening in the kingdom."

"What is that?"

"Have a celebration."

They both looked at her. Laurel smiled. "Perfect," she said.

"You think so?" said the king.

"Oh, yes!" cried Sylvie. "People need to be reassured, not frightened to death."

King Walther gazed at the tiny figures scurrying among the stalls, struggling to load their goods onto wagons.

"You may be right," he said.

"I know it," said Sylvie earnestly. "*You* know it."

"You are a good king," said Laurel, her dark blue eyes glowing.

That evening, long tables were set up inside the fortifications so that everyone, even the lowliest, could take part in the festivities. The peasants, who generally lived on dark bread and cheese, watched in amazement as servants set before them savoury pies, slabs of mutton, roasted cranes, spiced eels, spitted larks, mounds of dates and great pots of honeycomb.

After the sixth course, the king banged his flagon on the table and stood up to give a speech that brought tears to the eyes of everyone. Even Prince Riggeloff's voice sounded thick when he stood and proposed a toast to the gracious monarch and his family. Musicians and acrobats entertained the guests and then, as was becoming a tradition at royal celebrations, Sylvie's friend Laurel was asked to tell a story. When she finished, smiling her small smile, her head ducking in a little bow, everyone laughed and stomped and cheered. It was hours before the celebration broke up.

Morning dawned without a cloud in the picture-perfect sky and soon people were busy about their lives again, which meant hurrying to get to their places whenever a new Reader appeared overhead. During a free moment, Sylvie paused on the drawbridge and took her locket from around her neck. Usually, Laurel's face was inside, but not always. Sylvie flicked the locket open now and was surprised to see a pudgy boy sitting at a computer and tapping on a keyboard. He looked familiar, but she couldn't place him. Disappointed, she shut the locket.

Shortly after 9 A.M., Lulu began whimpering. The whimpering widened into howls and the little dog began running in circles. From a distant pasture, Sylvie heard the bleating of terrified sheep. Birds stormed out of the trees, circling, landing and immediately taking off again. Courtiers poked their heads out of window slots in the keep. Guardsmen notched their bows. Then, promptly at 9:14 A.M., the sky flickered as if from heat lightning, although the day was cool and clear. Suddenly, the sun blinked off and on, off and on, twice quickly, trading places with a full moon. This had never happened before, and the shepherds tending their flocks looked up in amazement, and were afraid.

Without warning, the air filled with the sound of manic beeps, high quick piping sounds coming from everywhere at once. Then a raucous crash of static, like thunder played backwards, overwhelmed everything else. Many people were terrified and clapped their hands over their ears. A lady-in-waiting fell to her knees, praying. Pingree held on to a stone pillar, as if expecting the ground to shake; but this was no earthquake, and as suddenly as it had begun, the roaring ceased. There were faint bells, as of distant connections being made, and then – strangest of all – a sensation of lightness in the pit of everyone's stomach.

The book was gone!

part two

Wordpool

Chapter Six

"Something's different," said Sylvie, who was gripping her father's hand on one side and Laurel's on the other.

"Very," said Laurel.

"I think I'm going to throw up!" groaned Pingree.

"Not me! I feel light!" cried Queen Emmeline, cradling her little brown-and-white Chihuahua in her arms. "I feel I could dance!"

"Yes, and something else," said Laurel.

"I know!" Sylvie exclaimed. "No smell."

"You're right," said the king, looking around. "The smell of the pages. Gone."

"Gone," echoed the queen.

"Because we're no longer in a book," Sylvie said.

"That must be why we feel lighter. The weight of the pages . . ."

"The pressure of the binding," Laurel added.

"The weight of the cover," said the queen. "Gone."

"I miss them," said Sylvie.

"Yes," said the king, looking around in wonder at the unchanged, yet wholly different, landscape.

"But I'm so light!" said the queen, still marvelling. "This heavy velvet gown – it's like nothing at all!"

"I can't feel my crown on my head!" The king reached up for it.

The first hour in the new world was filled with general hilarity as knights raced about in their feather-weight armour wielding spears as light as conductor's batons. Even the ladies-in-waiting – not known for agility – found they could easily jump over a description rather than struggle through it. The younger ones took turns leaping over word-thickets and tumbling harmlessly on the other side. Pingree, to his delight, was able to juggle nine oranges at once, where before he'd been able to manage only four.

"Let's go see what's happening!" cried Sylvie, and she and Laurel hurried down the stairs – almost fluttered down, so little did they feel the gravity that held them.

When they crossed through the market, they found everyone talking at once. The fish lady was loudest of all.

"I thought me cart was stolen!" she cried to the fruit seller. "I couldn't smell the fish no more!"

"Nor we couldn't smell you!" he shouted back, laughing. "'Where is Ursula the Fish Woman?' we asked. Didn't we, Mother?"

His wife laughed and bit into a yellow apple.

Everyone, in fact, seemed a little giddy. Not only had they survived; they were all suddenly light-footed, and this made them light of heart as well. Two pipers and a lute picker struck up a tune and soon several couples were whirling about in a high-stepping dance.

The giddiness ended abruptly when the first new Reader logged on and pulled up Chapter One. Suddenly, everyone felt a tug in the vitals, the way a fish might feel when aware of a hook. This inward twinge wasn't actually painful and lasted only a moment, but it was their first reminder of limits.

"It's like being on a leash," Sylvie said in disgust. "Now I know how Lulu feels when Mother trots her out for a walk."

"Shh," whispered Laurel, "we don't know enough yet."

"What's to know?" said Pingree, overhearing. "We had to run to get to our places before. Now we're being yanked there."

"Probably not everyone minds that," replied Laurel. "I would think the king would find it reassuring."

"Reassuring, not to be able to do what you want?"

"Life, Mr Pingree, is not about doing what you want."

The jester gave the girls a disgusted look and headed off to his next scene. He immediately fell down, got up and fell down again, because he wasn't used to the way the story moved in this new world. It wasn't easy for any of them. Instead of sitting on a page, the words moved slowly upwards, and the characters all had to step down from line to line as the Reader went on. Sylvie stumbled several times before she got the hang of it. It was like acting out their story on a moving staircase!

Queen Emmeline was having the worst time of all. She was used to planting her feet and making pronouncements, and couldn't get used to walking constantly downhill and saying her lines at the same time.

The long gown didn't help. It snagged on the tops of *t*s and *l*s. The capital *F* that starts page 37 was particularly treacherous, tearing a swatch of lace from her petticoat. After several tries, the queen learned to pick her way around the tall letters, and the story continued. But then the Reader clicked a small picture of an envelope in the lower left corner and disappeared.

Sylvie hadn't noticed that line of pictures before. There was another row of them across the top of the screen, like decorations bordering a window. Of course, everything was reversed on her side of the screen.

"What do we do now?" said Sylvie, who had been in the middle of her big confrontation with Prince Riggeloff.

"What *can* we do?" muttered the prince, scratching his beard.

Rosetta had been petting a lamb nearby. "We're still weightless," she noted, "so we must still be on-line. We're just not on-screen."

"What is that woman talking about?" rumbled Riggleoff. He had never warmed to the newcomer. "On *what* line? How long must we wait?"

In fact, they didn't wait long at all. With a squawk, a

bright bird sailed overhead, and then the sky lifted away. At the same moment, a sense of heaviness made Sylvie feel she was being pulled downwards by her very bones. The tall grass suddenly smelled like grass, and a gentle pressure on all sides gave her that old feeling of enclosure.

"We're back in the book!" she exclaimed.

Everyone was rushing about, many of them tripping over their suddenly heavy feet. Sylvie laughed, then immediately fell down. She got up, but noticed it took some effort. I can do this, she thought. Then she fell again. Having gotten used to stepping almost weightlessly down a scrolling page, she had to accustom herself all over again to the gravity of life in a paper-and-glue book.

"This is hopeless!" cried the king, as he stumbled into the throne room.

The characters managed to lurch through the first chapter, until the Reader, a towheaded boy of ten, was called away to lunch. The world went black, and a second later the back-up lights came on.

"Well!" cried the queen.

"Gravity," griped Pingree, "is vastly overrated!"

But by this time the girl on the Internet called the

story back onto the screen, and Sylvie instantly found herself in the midst of a towering argument with Prince Riggeloff. She was used to quick changes as Readers came and went, but this was especially tricky. Suddenly weightless, she had to fling angry retorts at the prince while stepping down the scrolling lines of dialogue. In the midst of it, she lost her footing and fell halfway down the screen. It would have been worse except that she grabbed the hook of the *f* in "furious" and regained her balance.

The Reader shook her head, perhaps thinking she had misread the sentence, which appeared to have a long *"Whoooaaaa!"* right in the middle of it.

So it went, book Readers and on-line Readers making their alternate demands on the bewildered characters. Then came the worst moment of all: a new on-line Reader yanked at them at the very moment that someone was opening the actual book! The simultaneous upward tug and downward pull made Sylvie feel she was being torn apart. She saw Pingree fall to his knees clutching his stomach. Queen Emmeline fainted.

The dreadful sensation lasted a couple of seconds, until a notice flashed onto the screen: **This Page**

Cannot Be Displayed. Sylvie caught just a glimpse of it before the force of gravity prevailed, siphoning everyone down into the book, where they struggled through their story as best they could.

In the course of that terrible first day, Sylvie realised she had left her locket in the on-line version of Chapter Six, on a rock overlooking the Mere, and in a free moment she ran to get it. Ran *down* to get it. Watching where she was stepping but not where she was going, she reached the bottom of Chapter Two and slammed into something that knocked her off her feet. It didn't hurt. In fact, it felt soft as stretched rubber; but it was invisible – an invisible wall. She tried to feel around its edges, but it had no edges. She could not leave!

For a scary moment, Princess Sylvie feared that she was trapped in Chapter Two. It was a fine chapter certainly, but you wouldn't want to spend your life there. And her locket! It was her most precious possession and it was lying, out of reach, in the middle of Chapter Six.

Not having any dialogue at the end of the chapter, Sylvie ducked behind a baneberry bush and waited for the Reader to catch up with her. She had been brought up to respect the main rule of storybook characters:

Never look at the Reader; but she regularly ignored that rule. The first thing she noticed, beside the tortoise-shell barrette in the Reader's long hair, was the fact that a transparent shield of some kind stood between them. In the book, there were no such separations.

She watched the Reader point a little arrow at a button marked (NEXT) and make a clicking sound that flung the characters into the following chapter.

There they were – instantly! In the book, nothing happened instantly. Time was something you could count on – not enough time, but some. Here, time didn't exist; or if it did, there were ways around it.

The week that followed was full of such revelations. She even learned how to go back the other way. The (BACK) button was on the bottom left, and if you kept pushing it, you could get from the end of the book all the way to Chapter One, if you wanted. Sylvie didn't have much time for such expeditions, but it was a relief to know that she could do it. She was especially glad to retrieve her octagonal locket. She vowed never to take it off again.

That first week was exhausting. Sylvie found her leg muscles twitching from the strain of constantly walking downhill. But mainly it was stress that wore the characters out. Rosetta had never been so busy coaching people on their deep-breathing technique. Now there was always a crowd waiting outside the anteroom where she taught.

Fangl had few duties in the story and was able to spend much of his time studying the way this new world worked. It wasn't easy, he found, to understand a machine from inside of it. There were many dark corners and, of course, no instructions.

"I've been listening to the Readers. They often mention a rodent that speaks in clicks and can transport a person to any part of the story instantly."

"Maybe that's the clicking sound we hear."

"It would appear so."

Sylvie shook her head in wonder. "But how do they train them?"

"I don't have the research on that."

"They sound pretty magical," said Sylvie, "if they can zip us from one part of the story to another."

"Magic," he said, "is just science we don't understand."

"I suppose."

"That golden octagon of yours, for instance." He nodded at the locket hanging from Sylvie's neck. "I'm sure there's a logical reason for everything it shows us."

"Wonderful, isn't it? You never know what you're going to see."

"Miss Laurel gave it to you?"

"Yes – to remember her by, she said. That was back when we weren't inside a book, and everything was chaotic, and we didn't know what was going to happen next."

Norbert Fangl looked at the princess. "It sounds like what's happening right now."

"You're right, Fangl. It's exactly like now!"

"May I ask, what did you see in it today?"

"Haven't looked." Princess Sylvie clicked open the delicate lid, then suddenly gasped and let go of the locket as if it were burning hot. It swung back and forth from its chain.

"What *is* it, Your Highness?"

Sylvie's face had gone pale. She held the locket by the edge and showed it to her tutor.

"Dear God!" he murmured.

Instead of the usual picture of Laurel, there was a turbulence of red, with occasional glints of yellow and black. Then the wild, slashing motions slowed, revealing a creature Sylvie and her tutor had never seen. It lifted its massive head as if sensing their presence through the locket, and opened its maw to let forth a soundless roar. The beast had leathery red scales, huge nostrils and insane-looking eyes. From its jaws, ropes of drool hung down.

Sylvie snapped the locket shut. She and Fangl stared at each other, unable to speak.

Chapter Seven

$\mathcal{P}$rincess Sylvie ran to find her friend Laurel, but once again she had disappeared. If anyone could understand the vision in the locket, she could.

Sylvie then climbed up to Rosetta's cottage, which was on a much steeper hill than before, since everything now moved vertically. She hadn't seen much of Rosetta since the uploading, except for classes and coaching sessions. The teaching was going well, and a special core of students had been making progress in their energy-projection exercises. There were four of these advanced students and they met with Miss Stein early in the morning, when Readers were few. This week they were learning to receive a line of energy from one person while they projected their own energy to another. It was very exciting. The quiet of dawn was often broken by the sound of electricity crackling like a whip.

No one answered her knock. Sylvie went round to the back and found the yoga instructor kneeling by the stream picking mint and watercress.

Sylvie nodded hello. "You understand this machine we're living in," she said. "Maybe you know why I've been seeing awful things inside my locket."

Rosetta stood up. "What things?"

"Horrible, terrible things. Here." Sylvie opened the locket and held it out.

Rosetta gave her a quizzical look. "Oh, I don't know," she said. "I think he's kind of cute."

"Cute?" Sylvie looked at the picture. It showed a little piglet scampering about in a sunny field. The only thing odd about it was its colour: bright green. "But there was a monster before!"

"Really? Maybe it has to do with all the electricity zooming around here on the Internet," said Rosetta. "Electronic interference or something. I wouldn't worry about it."

From what Sylvie could see, Rosetta didn't care very much about computers, although she had once studied them, she said, at school. Mint tea and watercress sandwiches were more interesting just now, and she invited Sylvie to join her for lunch. The two sat on a bench at the back of the house, talking and eating.

"That's one thing I don't like about being on the Internet," said Rosetta. "I can't smell the mint."

"You're right. Or taste it."

"You can't taste it?"

"Can you?"

Rosetta frowned. "I thought I could, until you said that. I can virtually taste it."

"Maybe what you're tasting is the memory of what it tasted like."

"Could you say that again?"

"Maybe you only think you can taste it."

"Hm. Maybe we only think we're sitting on a bench."

Sylvie rapped on it with her knuckles. "It certainly doesn't feel like wood."

Rosetta frowned. "At least it holds us up."

"Then again, we don't weigh very much here."

"It's a virtual bench."

"What about us? Are we virtual friends?"

Rosetta gave her a serious look. "I hope we can do better than that."

The two of them sat quietly chewing their tasteless sandwiches, until at the same moment they felt an uncomfortable tug in their stomachs telling them that a new Reader – or were they Viewers now? – had called up their story.

"Go to it, girl," said Rosetta, giving Sylvie a wink.

The princess ran off to relive her story. By now she got around pretty well, hardly stumbling at all as the text moved upwards. But then, during the scene in which King Walther voices his suspicions about Riggeloff, something happened that was totally bizarre. An enormous pink *ear* appeared, standing on end, trembling slightly, right there in the throne room! It was as tall as a man, with several dark hairs sprouting from the middle of it! Immediately afterwards, a thick fog rolled over the scene, obscuring everything.

"What's happening?" came the panicky voice of Queen Emmeline, who was feeling her way through the mist.

"Don't know!" the king called out. "I stepped in a soft spot and suddenly this, this gigantic . . ."

A servant rushed over with a torch, allowing the characters to see a little way in front of them. They could vaguely make out the ear, standing in the darkness like a monument.

"Father," said Sylvie in her quick voice, "what did you mean by 'soft spot'?"

"Here. Look."

They stared at an irregular discolouration, like a bruise, right there on the floor. It covered several sentences. Sylvie knelt. "Bring that torch closer," she said. The letters in the words were distorted, she saw, and even stranger—

"Father, the *d*s are missing!"

"What!"

It was true. When the king had stepped into that squishy place, his dialogue suddenly made no sense. That must have been why. The words, squirming slightly, lay before them:

"THERE'S SOMETHING WE NEE TO ISCUSS, EAR." SAI THE KING, FROWNING AT QUEEN EMMELINE. "THERE'S A TRAITOR IN OUR MIST."

"The mist! Of course!" King Walther exclaimed.

"And the ear!" put in Pingree, poking his head through the king's legs.

"But how do we get rid of it?" said the king.

"Quick," Sylvie said to one of the footmen, "run over to the Acknowledgments page and see if you can get us a few *d*s."

"Yes, Your Highness."

"No one reads that page anyway."

"No, Your Highness."

"*Small d*s. We'll need five of them."

The servant glanced at the king, who nodded. The man bowed and hurried off, returning with *d*s poking from all his pockets. But no one wanted to touch the jellylike place on the floor. The Chief Engineer and Mechanic was called to insert the letters. He scratched his greasy beard and tilted his head doubtfully. He wasn't able to make the sentences look right, but as soon as the letters were in place the mist cleared up and, to everyone's immense relief, the huge ear vanished.

"Well done!" King Walther grasped the man's dirty hand and shook it warmly.

News travels fast in a story, and soon characters were filtering in from nearby chapters to look at the soft spot in the text. "En't that sumpin'?" murmured the queen's chambermaid.

"You could throw a rug over it," suggested a

lady-in-waiting, elbowing her way through.

The king silenced them with a look. Poking with his sceptre, he found that the place remained treacherously soft, and he commanded it to be roped off. While the Chief Engineer worked, the only sound was the *whih-whih-whih* of the queen's fan as she sat on her throne looking faint.

"Things are getting interesting around here!" said Pingree, running his fingers through his straw-coloured hair and setting his jingling cap on his head. "I'll take this over a book any day!"

The queen gave him a horrified look, but didn't reply. *Whih-whih-whih* went her fan.

The king withdrew with his councillors for a special meeting. None of them had a convincing explanation for what had happened. One thought it was an accidental mix-up. Another wondered if this new world just had dangerous spots in it, the way their old world had bogs and quicksand. "The Mere has a wandering whirlpool that appears when you least expect it," he said. "Maybe it's like that."

"A wordpool," said King Walther. "Exactly!" He snapped his fingers for his scribe, who wrote a small neat sign:

DANGER!

WORDPOOL AHEAD.

KEEP OFF!

Several other councillors suspected that some sort of magic was involved. But who was doing it? There was no magician in the story. Yes, there were magical animals, and there was Godric's spell; but that spell had been placed on the prince before the story began – by the Author, one assumed.

"The only new person," said the Chief Councillor, pulling thoughtfully on his neatly pointed beard, "is that young woman, Miss Stein. What do we know about her?"

"Very little," the king conceded, "but surely . . ."

"Who else could it be?" cut in the oldest councillor, a waspish fellow with a brow that pitched forwards in a ledge that left his face in shadow. "Who? *Who*?" His voice was like a finger poking everyone in the chest. "No one, that's who. I say we arrest her!"

The others coughed and ahemmed and eventually voted him down. The truth was, they liked Rosetta Stein, with her windy hair. Being uploaded onto the Web would have been a much more nerve-racking business without her breathing techniques.

"And what are these exercises she's been giving all of you?" snapped the old councillor, who never took part in the lessons. He spat. "Magic, I say! Bad magic!"

In the end, the Council voted to keep Miss Stein under surveillance, but not to let her know it. This wasn't so easy to manage. The castle guards were good at clumping about and presenting arms, but untrained in the art of spying. A thief would be better, one who had no dialogue. But would he be reliable? The king finally hit upon Thomas, who was too good-natured to be much use as a thief and could easily be spared for this special duty. It was soon arranged.

In the meantime, the characters continued their exhausting routine of switching from the digital world to the print world and back again, often within a few minutes' time. Stress continued to be a problem, and if Miss Stein was suspected, she was also needed.

For his part, Thomas was happy with his assignment and kept a close eye indeed on the activities of Miss Stein. The knights continued to make a daily search for any other soft spots that might appear. After a week with no new sightings, the king began to think the "ear" episode was an accident that wouldn't recur.

Even Sylvie let her guard down a bit. She always glanced ahead at the upcoming lines of the story, but the plot moved so quickly she couldn't keep an eye on everything. A particularly fast stretch came in the chapter where the thieves are galloping after her, and she and her little donkey leap from the cliff into the Mere of Remind.

This time, as she raced on her donkey towards the approaching precipice, she suddenly caught a glimpse of a dark patch ahead. Before she could react, her donkey had splashed through it and made its fateful leap into the void.

A thrill of panic always gripped Sylvie during those seconds of free fall, but now there was an extra edge to her fear. That had been a soft spot! What did it mean? Would the water even be there when she landed?

It *wasn't!* She and the donkey separated in midair and slammed down onto something very hard but also smooth and slippery. Sylvie had the wind knocked out of her and wrenched her shoulder. She could not have got up, even if she weren't sliding helplessly along the shiny surface. As she began slowing down, she thought of her donkey, who must have been hurt. And where was the water? She had to get into the water before Riggeloff's men let loose their arrows! Painfully, she raised her head and squinted towards the cliff above her. There they were, Riggeloff, Hroth and the rest. Their taut bows were lifting. There would be no under-water escape this time.

Suddenly the air darkened as a volley of shafts whistled in her direction. She closed her eyes, knowing that not all the arrows could miss her. What a strange way for her story to end, she thought. She would die without understanding why, in a place that was her home and yet as alien as the moon.

"Ow!" Something pricked her arm and she opened her eyes to see flowers cascading down on her, their shafts poking her, their thorns making her wince. She was being assaulted with roses!

"What a great story!" she heard a girl's voice exclaim far above her. It was the Reader's round face in the sky where the sun should be. "The arrows turn into flowers!"

They do? Sylvie picked up a large rose and smelled it. No scent. Of course not. Prince Riggeloff and the thieves were looking down from the cliff in bewilderment. No one knew what to do, but they had to do something. There was a Reader overhead, and Readers expect a story.

Princess Sylvie felt a bumping beneath her and realised the invisible fish was trying to rescue her, but couldn't get through the surface. Glass, she realised, reflecting glass from shore to shore. Sylvie shook off the flowers, struggled onto her hands and knees, and finally to her feet. The donkey was not far away, favouring an injured forefoot as it hobbled towards her. The fall should have killed them both, but then, she realised, things weighed so much less in this world! Their lightness was what saved them.

Now she had to save her story. Clutching her sore ribs, she half hobbled, half skated to shore, picked up a jagged rock, and brought it back where she'd been. If the surface was glass, glass could break. She lifted the rock over her head and slammed it down with all her force. There was a loud pop and a cascade of clinks and clatters as the surface exploded and Sylvie fell through into the water, where the invisible fish dutifully swallowed her. The story went smoothly from there.

By the time the Reader closed the book, two chapters later, the Chief Engineer was at the scene, cordoning off the soft spot on the cliff. Fangl the tutor was there as well, examining the altered words. He had drawn a line around them in chalk.

"This time a whole paragraph has been changed," he said, as Sylvie limped over to him. "But in a different way."

"How?"

King Walther rode up with several knights. He quickly dismounted and took his daughter in his arms. "Sylvie!"

"I'm all right, Father. Just a little sore."

"Thank heavens! I could see you were hurt, and still you carried on."

"I had to. We had a Reader."

"That's why you're a heroine, my dear." He turned to Fangl. "What have you found?"

"Your Highness, look at this sentence here." He pointed to a misshapen group of words trembling on the ground like jellyfish:

PRINCESS SYLVIE AND THE DONKEY LEAPED FROM THE CLIFF AND FELL IN THE MIRROR.

"The mirror, Sire. They fell in the mirror!"

"I see." He didn't look as though he saw.

"You can't get from 'Mere' to 'mirror' by taking out a letter or two. The words aren't really similar in spelling; they're similar in *sound*. Here, look at this." He pointed to the next words:

THE THIEVES RAISED THEIR BOWS AND LET FLY A VOLLEY OF ROSES.

The king stared at the strange sentence. The words wiggled slightly as he read them.

"Again, Sire," said Fangl, "it's not the spelling. Taking out a letter will not get you from 'arrows' to 'roses'. It's the 'ro' sound in 'arrow' that leads you to 'roses'. Whoever's doing this obviously . . ."

The king's eyes widened. "So you agree with the councillors. You think someone is *doing* this?"

"Oh, yes. The chance of it being an accident is 332,820 to one. Give or take."

King Walther had begun gnawing on his moustache.

"My theory is that he – he or she – is trying out different approaches. The first was simple. This is more complex."

Sylvie and her father exchanged a long look. As

many challenges they'd faced within the covers of their book, they'd never come up against anything like this.

"Fangl," Sylvie said softly. She placed her small hand on his sleeve. "What do you think this person will try next?"

The tutor looked at her somberly, his eyes sadder than she had ever seen them. "Given the danger he was willing to put you in?" He shook his head. "I can't bear to think about it."

Chapter Eight

*A*t the next meeting of the council, the thief, Thomas, was brought in to give his report. He was happy to say that Rosetta had been nowhere near the cliff for at least a week. Still, the eldest councillor continued to suspect her. It seems an informant had told him about Rosetta's flare-up with Sylvie some weeks ago. Miss Stein (the informant said) felt she was being kept a prisoner and treated like a slave.

"A slave? She thinks that?" The ledge of the old man's forehead cast his eyes in darkness. This Stein woman certainly had a motive.

The informant, as the Reader will have figured out, was none other than Pingree the Jester, a person who never needed a motive to stir up mischief. He'd been feeling feisty since being "liberated," as he put it, from the confines of the book. Out here in cyberspace, anything could happen. Anything *was* happening. Pingree even took liberties with his dialogue – something strictly forbidden. With everything else going on, no one had time to correct him.

"She may have a motive," Fangl put in, "but did she have the means or opportunity?"

"The means?" the old councillor said.

"*Could* she have done it?"

The old man's forehead grew even more prominent as he thought about this. Apparently he did most of his calculating at the front of his brain. He turned to Thomas. "Young man, were there any times when the suspect was out of your sight?"

"Well," Thomas began, the tips of his ears reddening, "I didn't peek in her window when she went to bed at night."

"Aha!"

"Really!" Sylvie frowned at the old man.

"Excuse me, Thomas," said Fangl mildly, stepping forwards, "but were you keeping the house itself under watch all this time?"

"Every minute, sir."

"And is there only one door?"

"Only one, sir."

The old councillor raised a skinny eyebrow. "Are you *quite* sure?" he said, his voice insinuating. "*No* other exit?"

It was obvious that Thomas wanted Miss Stein to be innocent, but he had to admit that her window looked out from the rear of the house – a window he couldn't see from his place of concealment.

The old man said nothing, but Sylvie saw a vein pulsing in his protruding forehead.

King Walther cleared his throat. "Perhaps we could take a look at that window, when Miss Stein is busy elsewhere."

Sylvie looked from one to the other. "I hate this. It's sneaky!"

"My dear," said the ancient councillor, his eyes cold, "whoever is causing these accidents – which are no accidents at all – is far worse than sneaky!"

"Then why not suspect the people we already know are criminals? People like Prince Riggeloff."

Fangl shook his head. "Brilliant as the prince is," he said, "it is unlikely he would know about computers. I'm afraid our culprit is not anyone from the original story."

King Walther looked grim. "It has to be Miss Stein."

"*Now* will you arrest her?" cried the councillor.

"First, let's inspect that window at the back of her house."

Sylvie stood up. "I'll do it, Father. I'm responsible for her being here."

The king looked at her sadly. "Very well."

As the meeting broke up, everyone looked glum except the old councillor, who wore a tight smile that reminded Sylvie somehow of Pingree. They had a lot in common, those two.

Instinctively, she went searching for her friend with the dark blue eyes. Laurel was the smartest person she knew, and a smart person would be useful. But no one had seen the girl for days. Sylvie would have to face this on her own.

She put off going as long as she could. Finally, with a sigh, she trudged up the meadow's steep incline till she reached Rosetta's cottage. Glancing through the branches of a large sugar maple, she could just make out Thomas's legs hanging over the edge of a platform set high in the foliage. She gave him a half-wave and knocked at the door. After thirty long seconds, she knocked again. No response.

Don't let there be anything, she thought, heading round the back. But as she approached the window her heart sank. There was no mistaking the dried mud on the sill. She looked down. The heel of a narrow shoe had left a deep indentation in the earth, and the grass looked trampled.

Rosetta, don't do this. Don't be the one.

The window, unlatched, was the kind that swung outwards, and Sylvie pulled it open a few inches. "Anyone home?" she called into the darkness.

Why am I afraid? she thought. I'm the heroine. The truth was, she was afraid, terribly, of being disappointed in a person she thought well of. Besides, it went against her nature to sneak around like this. If ever there was a straight-forward character, it was Princess Sylvie. Here goes, she thought, and pulled herself over the sill.

She dropped inside and stood listening, the blood thudding in her chest. As her eyes adjusted to the dimness, she saw the table and the chair with the seat of woven straw. Vaguely visible on the ceiling was the drawing of constellations Rosetta had shown her. She stared at it. This was the wider view Rosetta used to have, Sylvie thought. Probably she drew it because she missed it. There was a universe beyond the confines of *The Great Good Thing*.

Confines. Yes, she could see how Miss Stein might consider herself a prisoner here. She didn't have an important role to play, or fine clothes to wear, or a decent house to live in. Why was she here? To be ordered around by other characters? This was a woman who had told her she *could not* be ordered around.

Sylvie began poking in the corners. She didn't want to light a candle; it would leave a smell that would tell Rosetta she had been here. Along one wall, Sylvie made out wooden pegs from which hung two shepherdess outfits. On a shelf lay a pot, a ladle and a few cups and plates. A kettle stood on the little stove, and a washbasin leaned against the wall behind the door.

Sylvie knelt down and felt under the cot. "Ack!" she cried as small clawed feet skittered over her hand. Swallowing hard, she reached under again, this time pulling out a pair of woollen slippers and a cloth bag. She held the bag up and shook it, listening to a soft clacking sound. That's odd, she thought, carrying it to the table near the window. The first thing she pulled out was a small hard object of white outlined in black.

It looked like a musical note, she thought, holding it by its stem. Seen another way, it looked like a small *p*. She turned it the other way round. It could be a small letter *b* as well. Or . . . she turned it over sideways. Or the letter *d*.

She emptied the bag. Four more objects, identical with the first, clattered onto the table.

"Oh!" she gasped, realising what she had found.

At that moment, the door banged open and a very angry Rosetta Stein stood staring at her, her hands on her hips. "Just what are you doing in my house!"

For a moment, Sylvie was speechless, her face flushed. Then she shook her head, remembering what she held in her hand. "What are *these* doing in your house?"

Miss Stein approached. Sylvie hadn't realised how much taller a tall grown-up was than a twelve-year-old girl. Rosetta's eyes flashed. "I thought better of you. I didn't think you would sneak into my house."

"I didn't think you would sneak *out* of it!"

"What are you talking about?"

Sylvie stood her ground. "Look at the mud on the windowsill. Look at the ground below it. If you had nothing to hide, why not go out by the front door?"

"Why don't *you* go out by the front door? Right now." Miss Stein's voice was still low, but it held a threat.

"All right," Sylvie replied. She strode across the room; but then she paused, her hand resting on the latch. "I think you should talk to me. If I go out of that door, the soldiers will come and arrest you."

"Arrest me?" Miss Stein seemed genuinely surprised. "Why?"

"Why? Look at what's lying on that table."

"Those ornaments?"

"Ornaments! No, they're the letter *d!*"

Rosetta looked at them. "Are they? Well, all right, they're the letter *d*. I found them in the stream and thought they'd make nice decorations."

"What?"

"I thought I'd string them together and hang them by the window."

"Rosetta, this is serious. Those letters were stolen from Chapter Three."

"Stolen? Who would do that?"

"That's the question, isn't it? Maybe somebody who was angry. Maybe somebody who thought she was a prisoner in this story, and was treated like a slave."

Rosetta sat down in the chair.

"It would have to be somebody," Sylvie continued, "who knows about computers. Nobody here does. Except you."

"I see. First a prisoner, then a slave, now a criminal."

Sylvie said nothing.

"This is turning into quite a delightful adventure you've arranged for me."

"Why did you do it? To get back at me?"

"I didn't do anything!"

"Then why have you been sneaking out of the window?"

"I don't like the tone of that."

"I don't either; but you can tell me or you can tell the king. He's the one who sent me."

"The king sent you!"

"Rosetta, just tell me."

The young woman and the girl stared at each other hard; then Rosetta closed her eyes and took a deep breath. She expelled it slowly and took another. After the third she opened her eyes. "Okay. It's simple. Let me say, I do think that fellow Thomas is harmless, but he can be awfully persistent."

"Thomas?"

"He follows me everywhere. Even when I'm at home he sits up in that tree at the front and watches. Back where I come from, we have a name for people like that."

"I see."

"There are times a girl wants to be watched, as you must know, Sylvie. And there are times she can't *stand* to be watched. When I feel like that, I leave him sitting up in his tree while I climb out at the back."

"And where do you go?"

"Wherever I please."

Sylvie nodded. She could understand wanting to go where one pleased. "Was one of those places the cliff over the Mere of Remind?"

"Sure."

"When were you there last?"

"A few days ago. It's one of my favourite spots."

Sylvie closed her eyes for a moment to think of a good way to say this. "While you were there, did you do anything to the words of the story? Change them around? Take out a few letters?"

Rosetta's eyes narrowed. "Why would I do that?"

Sylvie sighed. "I don't know. I'm sure you didn't mean to hurt my donkey."

"Your donkey was hurt?"

"He landed pretty hard. He's all right now."

Rosetta shook her head. "I'm afraid you've lost me completely."

"What did you *think* would happen when you turned the Mere into a mirror?"

"I did *what*?"

"You deny it?"

"Of course!"

Sylvie lifted one of the *d*s, weighed it in her hand, and let it drop on the table with a soft *clunk*. "And you just found these in the stream?"

"In the stream, yes."

Sylvie put the letters in the bag. "Do you mind if I take them along with me?"

"Yes, I do mind." Rosetta stood up, and again Sylvie was aware how tall she was.

"The king needs to see them."

"Am I to be arrested?"

Sylvie found it hard to speak for a moment. This was incredibly painful. "Probably," she said.

"I can't believe this."

Sylvie looked out of the window at the distant stream and trees, then at the young woman she had hoped would be her friend. "Should we go together?"

"Why not?" Rosetta picked up the bag of *d*s. "Poor Thomas. What will he do without me to follow round?"

"Oh, he'll be sent back to rejoin the thieves." Immediately, Sylvie realised she had said the wrong thing.

"What! You mean he was *told* to spy on me?"

Sylvie again found herself speechless. She could see the pain in Rosetta's eyes.

"And I thought he was just an oddball who brought me irises and slipped poems under my door."

"I'm sorry."

"So much for vanity!" Rosetta put her hands together and tapped her lips with them. "And I suppose you've got some sort of dungeon in the castle."

"Well, yes."

"Is that where they plan to put me?"

"Just until the trial."

"The trial. After which I suppose I'll be drawn and quartered?"

"They don't do that any more."

"Prison reform! Thank goodness! Sylvie, help me. You used to be my friend."

"I want to be your friend."

"Then tell me what to do."

Princess Sylvie felt as miserable as her character was ever permitted to feel. There were no good choices for Rosetta Stein. "Do you happen to have any food?" she said at last.

"Are you hungry?"

"No, I'm not. Do you have a sturdy knife?"

"Yes."

"Good walking shoes?"

"Yes."

"Rosetta, I'm going to take a look at those constellations on the ceiling over here. I'm really interested in stars, so I'll probably be looking at them for five minutes or so."

For a moment, their eyes met with extreme clearness. Then Sylvie turned away and went to stand under the drawing on the ceiling. She heard Rosetta banging about, but didn't turn round. There was the sound of something being dragged, the shushing of fabric, the creak of the window opening. She heard another scrape, then a thump, then nothing.

Chapter Nine

*N*ews of Rosetta's disappearance whizzed through the hyperlinks and pixels, and before the morning was out everyone was talking about it. King Walther and his advisors were used to dealing with villains, but they'd never had an outlaw before. At first, detachments of soldiers were sent to search for her; but *The Great Good Thing* was too popular for them to leave for long. No sooner did the men ride off into the forest than they had to gallop back again, because a boy in Weehawken or a retiree in Boca Raton had just clicked onto the story.

Queen Emmeline was thoroughly befuddled. She wasn't good at dividing her attention this way, and she sometimes made embarrassing slips. King Walther had problems of his own. As he finished his rousing speech to the soldiers in Chapter Seven, he was suddenly pelted with buckets of thick green mush. Later was it discovered that the "wild applause" he usually received had been changed to "wild *applesauce*".

Not even Princess Sylvie was immune to disasters. Her touching last scene with Prince Godric was ruined when Sylvie was suddenly engulfed in a cloud of insects. Soon she was rolling about on the ground, itching uncontrollably. Fangl examined the text and found that "trees" had been changed to "fleas".

After leaping in the water to escape the biting insects, Sylvie found herself thinking, Is this the thanks I get?

That thought upset her more than the fleas had done. I must really think she did it! Who else had a motive? Who else knew how to use a computer?

Rumours about the fugitive raced from peasants to courtiers and back. Some said Miss Stein had been seen entering the thieves' hideout; others heard that she was in the invisible fish at the bottom of the Mere. One thing was certain: She was not in the kingdom any more. The courtiers missed their yoga sessions; Godric was distraught; Thomas was glum.

Sylvie decided to look for Rosetta herself. After

midnight, when Readers were few, the princess slipped a chunk of bread in the pocket of her green cape, mounted her donkey and trotted into the forest. Moonlight struggled through the trees, casting patterns of black and silver on the dusty pathway. Overhead, the blind owl soared, hunting for prey, its dark wings tipped in light. A large mound lay nearby, and Sylvie recognised it as the great tortoise, its head and legs withdrawn for the night. There was no sense looking out for wordpools, she realised. They wouldn't be visible in the half-light. She also decided not to call out. Why alert the wolves that a young girl was travelling alone through the wilderness? Her presence might already have been sensed, to judge from a distant howl that reached her from the other side of the hill.

"Come on," she murmured to the donkey. It, too, had heard the howl, and was hesitating. "Don't worry," Sylvie said, "stories always turn out in the end."

She looked ahead along the rising path. Just where it turned and disappeared in the trees, she caught a glimpse of – something. The creature was gone before she could see it clearly – an animal, perhaps, crossing in the moonlight. She gave her donkey a nudge with her heels.

When they reached the bend in the path, Sylvie dismounted, listening hard. Off in the bushes about ten yards, she heard a rustling.

"Rosetta?" she said in a loud whisper.

The sound stopped abruptly. Sylvie didn't breathe. Two silences listened.

"Is that you, Rose?"

The silence tightened. Something was there in the bushes by the large pine tree. Sylvie picked up a sharp stone.

"I'm coming over," she said in what she hoped was her normal voice. Twigs snapped underfoot as she left the path. The bushes trembled.

"*Yaaaahhh!*" A creature burst up with a scream and scampered away like a deer, but manlike, on two legs, around the back of the pine.

Sylvie clapped her hand to her throat. When her breath returned, she gripped the stone hard and moved slowly towards the tree.

"Come out of there!" she shouted, trying to put menace in her voice.

The creature suddenly flitted to a different tree and

again disappeared. This time Sylvie caught a glimpse of ragged clothing and sunburnt skin. The creature was human, she realised, and more afraid than she was.

"I won't hurt you," she said, more softly. "Please come out."

For long seconds there was no sound or movement. Then, slowly, the sorriest-looking man she had ever seen rose to his feet. His eyes looked pale in his sun-blackened face, and what clothes he wore seemed patched together from old pieces of canvas, small sticks and bits of string.

"Who are you?" said Sylvie.

"Gunn, Miss."

The name meant nothing to her. "Are you lost?"

"Marooned," he said. "Marooned three years agone." His voice sounded as if he hadn't used it for a long time. "Might ye have something to eat, Missy? Something for poor Ben Gunn?"

Sylvie felt in the pocket of her cape and pulled out the hunk of dark bread. She broke it and reached out with the larger half. Gunn snatched the bread and lunged into it while she watched him. "Where are you from?" she said when he had finished.

"From *Treasure Island,* by the powers," he said.

"I don't know that place."

"'T ain't a place. 'T'sa book!"

"What!" She remembered her conversation with Norbert Fangl, when she'd learned about the existence of other books. "You really *are* lost, then," she said.

"Yes'm, that I am, Missy, I'll lay to that!"

"Come here where we can sit down. Let's talk a bit."

The wretched man hitched up his brass-buckled belt, but didn't move.

"I'll give you more bread."

He moved closer, suspicion vying with hunger.

"Come," she said, sitting down and patting the ground beside her.

He nodded and crouched on his haunches a few feet away. She held out the bread, and he grabbed it. By the time he had finished and licked the last crumbs from his dirty palms, Ben Gunn was in a more talkative mood. But he didn't have much to tell. One moment he was seeking shelter from the broiling sun on a remote island, and the next he was in a forest at night, with a chill wind blowing through his rags.

Had he seen nothing, heard nothing, between the first scene and the second?

"Just the laugh, is all."

"The what?"

"As cold a laugh as ever I heard from Long John Silver. A cackle, like. Except this weren't no man laughin'."

"A woman's laugh?" said Sylvie, suddenly dreading his answer.

Ben Gunn thought, then slowly shook his tangled locks. "Nor no woman, neither. A youngster. Girl or boy I can't say."

Sylvie saw that Gunn was shivering. The switch from desert island to northern forest must have been a shock. "Here," she said, taking off her beautiful green cloak and draping it around his skinny shoulders. "Take this."

Gunn looked confused. "By the powers!" he said, his face brightening. "You're young, but you're right as paint." He grasped her hand roughly and squeezed it.

"Stay here now, Ben Gunn," said Sylvie. "I'll try to find a way to get you back to the book where you belong."

She hurried to her donkey, who was nibbling leaves by the path. "Come on, little one." She swung onto its back and gave it a nudge towards home. The animal needed no encouragement.

The mystery of Gunn's appearance in the forests of *The Great Good Thing* bothered Sylvie all night, and the next morning, after a fitful sleep, she set off to find her father. The chamberlain informed her that the king was not presently in the castle. He and the reeve who managed these lands had ridden to the lower pasture to examine the latest soft spot in the text.

Sylvie hurried through the outer courtyard, past the poultry pen and blacksmith's hut, to the drawbridge. Outside, there were more booths, with peasants hawking pots, tools, bags of grain and every kind of food. The street was crowded with fishmongers and farmers' wives. Sylvie knew many of the tradespeople and always stopped by the apple seller whenever she went out. This morning the usually cheery fellow was not smiling. He raised a heavy eyebrow as she picked out an apple.

"Have ye noticed the strangers, Your Highness?" he said in a muted voice.

"Strangers?"

He gave a sideways nod at a man standing near the back of the crowd. If this was a knight, he was wearing the most peculiar suit of armour Sylvie had ever seen. On his head, instead of a plumed helmet, he wore what appeared to be a funnel!

Sylvie took a bite of her apple for courage and walked up to the man. "Excuse me, Sir Knight," she said. "I couldn't help noticing . . ."

He interrupted her with a great sigh. "I'm afraid I'm all turned around. I was on another road just before. Can you point me in the right direction?"

At least he's polite, she thought. "This is the only road that leads out of town."

His neck squeaked like unoiled metal as he turned his head to look down the road. "The one I was on wasn't cobblestones," he said. "It was yellow bricks."

"I'm afraid we don't have any road like that."

Just then a great commotion made Sylvie wheel round. An outlandish looking vehicle, not like any coach or carriage she had ever seen, was jouncing and clattering down the cobbled street. Bright red and yellow, it bore the legend, "Neighbourhood Trolley," along its side. Dogs and children ran after it as it roared on, finally disappearing in the pine woods. Queen Emmeline's lapdog, Lulu, scrambled after the others, yapping madly.

"Lulu! Get back here! My goodness!" cried Sylvie. "I really must find Father!" Forgetting even to say good-bye to the knight in tin armour, she hurried down the road. By the time she had reached the patch of pine trees separating the town from the peasants' farms, the dust had settled and there was no sign of the trolley or of Lulu. They couldn't have gone far, she thought, continuing on.

Breaking out of the woods, she could see the king some fifty yards ahead, standing in a field of lettuce with the reeve and the peasant who tilled the land. Just as she was about to call out, Sylvie heard the familiar cry of a bright orange bird: "Reader! Reader!" and suddenly she was clicked away to a different part of the story altogether. One thing about cyberspace, you don't have to run to get to your place. The Reader calls up the chapter he wants, and there you are.

This Reader clicked onto the next-to-last chapter in the book. The thieves have burst into the castle's chapel, where the royal family has taken sanctuary: *Burly Hroth, his sword still smoking from battle, advanced on the king. Brecka, McGettigan, Flanner and Wratche had drawn their swords as well. King Walther, weaponless, backed slowly towards the altar, keeping the queen and*

Princess Sylvie well behind him. All at once, Prince Riggeloff strode into the room, his arms crossed before him and his eyes darting about dangerously.

"*I see we forgot some of the treasure,*" *he said, noticing a gleaming chalice and gold candlesticks on the altar.* "*Never mind. Your daughter would not have me. Now I'll have your whole kingdom!*"

"*Take it,*" *said the king, drawing himself up.* "*Take what you please.*"

"*No!*" *Sylvie's voice rang out. She stepped in front of King Walther. In her hand she held*

crashed against the wall. Cries of alarm echoed through the chapel as shards of glass rained down from the stained-glass windows above.

"What?" said Riggeloff, looking around. "What happened? There are four sentences I'm supposed to say in there!"

The king and queen exchanged glances.

Sylvie hurried over to the ragged edge of text and peered into the hole. "Looks like most of a paragraph is missing!"

"Careful, everyone!" the king said, looking around. "Don't go near it. Someone call the Chief Engineer."

"I'll get him," piped Thomas, setting off at a run.

Sylvie suddenly remembered that there was a Reader, who must be as confused as everyone else, but by then the Reader had already logged off.

"The reeve and I were just in the lettuce field," the king was telling the others. "That's another danger spot."

"Your Majesty?"

King Walther looked up at the sound of Laurel's voice.

"You're back!" Sylvie cried in relief.

"Yes," said the girl with the dark blue eyes. She shot Sylvie a small smile. "I've been trying to learn about these machines."

"What have you discovered, my dear?" King Walther said.

"Well," she said, "it seems we have a virus."

The characters looked at one another. "A what?" said Queen Emmeline.

"But I feel perfectly well," said the king.

"We are all well," said Laurel in her quiet voice. "It is our story that is sick. And it's getting worse."

"Worse," echoed Pingree. In spite of himself, he smirked. "To me, it's getting better! This old story has never been so much fun!"

"You'll see how much fun it is, Pingree, when you fall in a hole and disappear," snapped Sylvie.

"A virus," said Laurel, "can tear a story apart."

Just then, the castle and everything else was replaced by a starry night sky, with meteors heading right towards the characters and veering off at the last moment.

"Aii!" cried the queen, ducking down.

"Don't worry," came Laurel's calm voice. "It's just somebody's screensaver. All you have to do is push any button and it goes away. There!"

The stars were gone, the castle was back and Laurel was standing by the scroll-up control.

"You mean," said the king, "that's not part of the virus?"

129

"Fortunately not, Sire. Not harmful at all."

"A bit confusing, though."

"Yes, Sire."

Through the chapel window, the sound of bullfrogs could be heard, announcing, "Boook Ooopen! Ooopen!"

"We're not ready!" the queen exclaimed.

"Watch your steps, everyone!" warned the king. "Keep an eye out for soft spots."

"And holes!" the Chief Councillor called out.

And so, with everyone on edge, including the dog, Lulu, who was *always* on edge, the story began again. Besides the usual difficulties, there were a dozen roped-off areas to avoid, some of them in highly inconvenient places. Characters in a popular book are nothing if not professional and they carried on. Animals, on the other hand, are less professional. During the midnight scene in which the prince and his retainers sneak into the castle and toss Shawls of Slumber over the guards, Lulu suddenly scampered in and began nipping at Riggeloff's ankle. Sylvie, who was watching the scene from the side, couldn't help smiling as the prince tried to shake the animal off, all the while whispering his evil plans to his lieutenant, Hroth.

One after another, the guards succumbed as the gauzy Shawls of Slumber settled over their heads. Soon all were asleep. Hroth and his crew found the corridor leading to the treasure room . . .

"Get this wretched dog off of me!" Riggeloff was shaking his foot violently.

Silently, they drew their swords. Hugging the sweating walls, they crept forwards.

"Wow-yowyowyow!"

Just ahead lay the treasure room, its great iron door standing open. "It could be a trick, Sire," whispered Hroth.

Riggeloff's face darkened. "True enough," he muttered. "Shall we turn back then? Shall we retreat when the treasure of the kingdom awaits us through that open door?"

"No!" came Brecka's deep-edged voice.

"On with it," said McGettigan, his eyes glinting.

The others nodded. Riggeloff gave a crooked jerk to his lips, the closest he came to a smile, and signalled the men to follow.

The castle was deathly silent . . .

"Wow-yowyowyow!" yapped the bulgy-eyed dog, facing the men, jumping backward, turning in tight circles. "Wowowowow!" Suddenly, the dog raced ahead down the hallway and slipped through the open doorway.

... *Even the walls seemed to be listening. Riggeloff reached the end of the corridor. Before him, gleaming faintly, lay the*

Sylvie blinked. From her place on the side of the

page she could see nothing, a nothing that stretched forwards to the very end of the chapter. Riggeloff and his men stood at the doorway of the treasure room, but there was no treasure room, only emptiness. Lulu had disappeared. And from somewhere far away, beyond the borders of the story, came echoes of the coldest, most frightening laugh that Sylvie had ever heard.

part three

Paragon

Chapter Ten

"Lulu!"

Silence. Lulu was hardly ever silent.

"Lulu! Come, Lulu!" Queen Emmeline stood by the empty place and called out, her voice echoing.

Princess Sylvie looked at Norbert Fangl. He compressed his lips and shook his head. The place seemed less like a hole in the story than an absence, a nothing-at-all. And now the little brown-and-white dog was part of it.

"Lulu!" Tears stood in the queen's eyes. "Where are you?"

"It might make sense," suggested Laurel, "if we split up to look for her."

The king nodded, not really listening. His arm was round his wife's shoulder.

"Why don't you come with me, Princess?" Laurel gave a little pull on Sylvie's sleeve.

"Um, sure."

The two friends left the castle and headed into the pine forest. They stopped by a large hemlock amid the gloom of rhododendrons.

"Do you think we'll find Lulu out here?" Sylvie said.

"No, but I wanted to talk to you."

"What is it?"

"Before you go on your expedition, I should tell you what I've learned."

"What makes you think I'm going on an expedition?"

"Because you want to save the book," said Laurel. "That's the way your character is written. But you don't know what you're up against."

Sylvie looked at her friend, the wisest person she knew, and saw something she'd never seen before: a suggestion of fear.

"You're going to need help," Laurel said.

"Well, I have you."

"Yes, you have me. But you'll also need Fangl; and you'll need Rosetta. She may not be enough either. Nothing may be enough."

"But Rosetta has disappeared."

"I've hidden her."

Sylvie could only stare. Her friend's act was a direct disobedience of the king. "Can you take me to her?"

"Yes."

"Where is she?"

"Right here. And yet separate."

"You're always so mysterious."

"It's true, though. The king's men could search the kingdom for a year and not find her."

"Yet you say she's here?"

Laurel nodded. "While I was gone this last time, I learned a great deal. I told you that I watch over my family. Claire's brother has died, but his son has a family, three thirteen-year-old daughters and a boy named Ricky, who is – different."

"What do you mean?"

"Ask Lily about him some time. She's his long-suffering aunt. Anyway, all of them use computers, and I've looked over their shoulders quite a bit. It really helps to see these things from the outside."

"That's what Fangl used to tell me. You can't solve a problem from inside it."

"I like your Mr Fangl. By the way, did you know about the 'Help' button?"

"No."

"Very useful. You can see it there on the upper right. Did you also know that you can move things around?"

Sylvie shook her head.

"It's a trick I learned from watching Lily's nephew, Ricky. Mostly he's playing some strange computer game, but he knows a lot. More than the others."

"What does this have to do with Rosetta?"

"Well," she said, "I've moved *her* around."

Sylvie looked blank.

"Here, I'll show you." She hopped onto the scroll bar on the side of the screen and took it, like a tiny lift, to the top. Jumping off, she clambered over a number of tiny pictures, then reached down and gave a quick pound with her fist. Suddenly the forest disappeared, and there was nothing but whiteness.

"What did you just *do*?" called Sylvie.

Laurel started to climb down, using the vertical ruler on the left as a stepladder. "I've moved *us* around."

"And we're out of the story?"

"We're in it, but we're hidden."

Sylvie looked across the screen. It was like being in an all-white room without a stick of furniture. Then, in the lower corner, she saw a woman dressed like a shepherdess, sitting cross-legged with her eyes closed.

"Rosetta!"

The woman looked up. "It's you," she said.

Sylvie ran to her. "I was so worried!"

Rosetta couldn't hide her smile. "You don't still think I'm the cause of all your problems?"

"Oh no, not at all!"

"That's a relief."

"For one thing, all kinds of strange things have been happening since you've been tucked away in here." Sylvie told about her experience with the outlandish Ben Gunn, then about the strange-looking knight with the tin funnel on his head.

Laurel and Rosetta glanced at each other. "Sounds like other stories are leaking in," said Rosetta.

"Or they're being *put* in," added Laurel. "And now, great hunks of the story have been erased!" A look of sadness came over her. She sat down, leaning against the white background, and closed her eyes. "My beautiful story," she murmured, touching her hand to her forehead.

"What did you say?" said Sylvie.

Laurel seemed not to have heard her.

"You said, 'my story'."

"Did I?"

"You mean, you *wrote* it?"

Laurel looked at the princess and smiled slightly. "Of course I wrote it. You knew that."

"I didn't!"

"You didn't want to know it, but you did. You kept stepping back from knowing it." Laurel looked from Sylvie to Rosetta. "I learned a lot of things since I died. I learned that we make our own heaven. This has been mine."

"To live in this story?"

"Yes, with my favourite characters – with you, Sylvie – and be the age I was when I wrote it."

"How," Sylvie began, placing her small hand on her chest, "how can I talk to you? You *created* me."

"Yes," Laurel said softly. "But don't make more of it than it is. I always felt this book was a gift. It came to me somehow, and I just wrote it down."

Sylvie shook her head, hardly believing what she was hearing. "I should have realised," she murmured. "You said you were the book's first Reader. Of course you were!"

She sat down beside the others, the three of them

leaning against the white background and looking at that moment like a row of dolls on a shelf.

"You must have really hated having *me* come into the story," said Rosetta.

Laurel nodded. "It took some getting used to."

They sat in silence. "What can we do?" Sylvie said at last.

Rosetta was tapping her nose with her finger. "If someone has planted a virus," she said, "you're going to have to find him. Or her, of course."

"Hard to do," said Laurel. "You have to use a keyboard, which we don't have access to, and put words in, and go from link to link . . ."

The young shepherdess pursed her lips. "That's true. We have links *within* our story – getting from one chapter to another – but no way out."

"Are you saying," said Sylvie, getting to her feet, "that in order to get out you have to *be* out?"

"Okay, okay," Rosetta said. She, too, got to her feet and began pacing, her long hair swerving behind her. She and Sylvie passed each other while Laurel looked up at them. "Let's think about this. First of all, the book does exist outside of the Web, doesn't it? We've had to go back and forth often enough."

"That's true," said Sylvie.

"So even if this world disappears, the story wouldn't be totally lost."

"That's something," said Laurel.

"That's a great deal," said Rosetta firmly. "We'll still be okay whatever happens."

"Well, it doesn't *feel* okay," said Sylvie, "when you're jumping off a cliff and there's no water below you."

"I suppose what's depressing," said Laurel, "is knowing that someone out there *wants* to destroy us, is trying very *hard* to destroy us."

"I know," said Rosetta.

"It's the meanness of it."

"Why didn't I think of this?" Sylvie cried suddenly. "There *is* a way out and one of the characters has already taken it."

"Who are you talking about?" said Laurel.

"I'm talking about Lulu."

"No! I won't let you!" Laurel was standing, too. Suddenly the white room seemed very small.

"Now you're sounding like my father."

"I made you. I'm not going to lose you."

"Laurel, listen. Whoever is trying to destroy our story has been doing a good job of it. But nobody's perfect. He left a hole in the Web."

Rosetta's face lit up. "An escape hatch!"

"Exactly."

"Sylvie," she said excitedly, "you've got to let me go with you! I'm not doing any good here."

Princess Sylvie shook her head. "Thank you, Rose, but think about it. There's no sense risking two of us." She turned to Laurel. "If you don't mind, could you show me how to work that button, so I can get on my way?"

Laurel seemed on the verge of refusing, but then she looked at Sylvie and realised that her wonderful character would never take no for an answer. "I knew you'd be going," she said with a little sigh. "I just didn't know how you'd manage it."

Before long, the princess stood at the edge of The Great Deletion, as the other characters had already named the place. It had been roped off and a sign attached warning people away. The treasury door was swinging loosely back and forth on its hinges, keeping no one in or out.

Sylvie hesitated. Once she went through there, could she ever get back? Would she exist at all?

Don't do it. Save the story from where you are!

Sylvie shook her head to dispel the thought. "Okay, Lulu," she whispered under her breath, "I'm coming."

She climbed over the guard rope and stood listening to her heart bumping in her chest. Then she took a deep breath, lifted her chin and walked straight ahead, her blue shoes clicking down the empty hall.

Chapter Eleven

$\mathcal{D}$arkness closed over her. Sylvie glanced back in time to see the brightly lit world of *The Great Good Thing* grow smaller and smaller till it became a blue dot, like Earth seen from a star, and disappeared. So she was moving, then. She didn't feel she was. No breeze fanned her; no trees or buildings flitted past. She was flying blind.

Flying? Yes, she realised, or floating. She was no longer using her feet. If she was falling, she did not feel she was falling *down*. How else did one fall?

Before long, she detected a far-off glimmer tilting through the darkness. It was impossible to judge its size or distance; it might have been a galaxy, or simply a ship with its lights on. As it came closer, she realised the light wasn't as bright as she'd first thought. It was, in fact, a huge, dim honeycomb of passageways, like an empty hive, and she was heading right towards it. Instinctively, she twisted her shoulder to the left to avoid knocking into the side of the entrance, and she felt her body swerve to the left. Then she was inside, hurtling through greyish brown light. The corridor bent to the right and she twisted that way, discovering with relief that she had turned the corner. Now, if she could only slow herself down. . . . The walls on either side were lit by milky rectangles, and she wanted to look at them more closely.

Slow down, she told herself. To her astonishment, the illuminated panels came by more slowly than before. Was it possible she could control her speed by her thoughts?

Speed up! The lights began whizzing past.

A feeling of elation filled her. Left! she thought, coming to a crossroads in the labyrinth. She swerved neatly to the left.

The strangely lit rectangles came by every few seconds and provided the only light in the maze. Stop! she commanded, and came to a gentle halt in front of one of the panels. Vague light shone through the cloudy glass, behind which she could make out shapes. Sylvie reached out and touched the panel, and it sprang open, revealing a room filled with twirling wooden blades set in shiny brass mountings. A smiling woman — clearly a drawing — was speaking to no one in particular about something called "ceiling fans". Along the side wall, one above the other, were small blue signs marked OPTIONS, MORE INFORMATION and HOW TO ORDER.

"My goodness!" whispered Sylvie, quietly closing the door again. With a soft *shuck!,* a small plastic tray slid out beside the panel. A round glowing object lay upon it, bright yellow. Sylvie looked closer. It was a cookie, a delicious-looking lemon cookie lightly dusted with sugar! Then came a little ratcheting sound and out of a slot slid a small paper ticket. Sylvie tore it off.

> Thank You
> for Stopping By.
> Have a Nice Day!

"Isn't that lovely!" Sylvie lifted the cookie and took a small bite. "Achhh!" It was awful — no taste at all! — and made of some kind of soft plastic. It was worse than Rose's watercress sandwiches.

Sylvie floated to the next rectangle and touched it lightly. That panel, too, sprang open, and a cool salt breeze sailed out, filling the corridor. Sylvie stared in amazement at crashing surf and a tall red lighthouse rising from a rocky shoreline. LIGHTHOUSES OF NEW ENGLAND, proclaimed a sign that seemed to hang, without any support at all, in the blue sky. As she watched, a seagull flew up and perched on the letter *N* in NEW. It stared back at her, fluffed its feathers, and let out a sharp cry. Sylvie let the door close.

> Thank You
> for Stopping By.
> Have a Nice Day!

She made sure not to touch the cookie.

Door after door opened at Sylvie's touch as she floated down the corridors of the maze, and each one left her a thank-you note and a cookie. Before long, she could look back and see a row of glowing cookies stretching behind her.

One of the rectangles emitted a dull reddish light. What could this be? thought Sylvie, reaching out. A spark jumped at her fingers. "Ow!" she cried, jerking her hand away. No cookie this time. Just a little ticket that read:

> Warning! Firewall!
> Don't Even *Think*
> of Coming Here
> Again!

"Don't worry!" said Sylvie, rubbing her hand.

As she went on, she found more of these red, electrified doors. Naturally, she was curious to know what lay behind them. Why would anyone have a door and not let people enter it?

That didn't seem important now, when there were so many bright portals that actually welcomed her. For someone who had lived all her life in a medieval castle, it was a revelation to learn about package holidays to Hawaii; instruction in Japanese calligraphy; the proper tools to use when carving ice sculptures; and lizards of the American Southwest. If only the cookies tasted better!

She realised she couldn't possibly open all the doors, and for a while was content to float through the greyish silence of the corridor. A distant sound reached her, and she strained to hear. It was a faint, hoarse-sounding voice, calling, "Ow, ow, ow."

"Lulu!" she cried, speeding up. After two left turns, she found the barking had grown fainter, and she reversed herself, turning right instead. Yes, the sound was a little louder.

"Wowowow!"

"Lulu!" Sylvie cried. "I'm coming!"

But after several more turns, the barking had grown faint again. Sylvie stopped and reached for the golden locket that hung from her neck. Maybe it would give her a hint. Holding it in front of her face in the dim light, she clicked it open. At first she saw nothing. Then she flinched back as a yellow-eyed dragon reared its head before her. Hanging from its mouth and dripping with green saliva were several pages torn from a book.

Sylvie snapped the locket closed, her breath coming fast. Somewhere, in the heart of this great labyrinth, a monster waited for her. And in some way that she didn't understand, this creature was tearing her story apart.

The sound of distant barking caught Princess Sylvie's attention, and she pushed ahead, rounding turns, doubling back, racing on. The least she could do was rescue her mother's dog.

Two turns later, the barking was suddenly louder. Sylvie pulled up before a bright panel. She could see the shadow of a dog jumping up and down.

"Yip-yip! Rrrrrr!"

At a touch, the panel opened to bubbles, kazoos, braying trumpets and steel balls going *ding-ding!* as they rebounded in all directions. In the midst of it, a little dog was barking uncontrollably at a feathered rhinoceros.

"Lulu!" Sylvie stepped inside and scooped up the frantic dog. "There you are!" Lulu squirmed around in Sylvie's arms, yapping and nuzzling by turns.

A feathered rhinoceros?

Sylvie looked up at the huge thing, which had begun snorting and pawing the ground, its little red eyes glaring. What was this place? Arching overhead, a great banner proclaimed:

MELVIN'S MAGICAL MONSTERS!
ARCADE GAMES GALORE!

The beast lowered its head as if about to charge.

"Get away!" Sylvie shouted.

The animal continued snorting and pawing and occasionally lowering its head, but it wasn't looking particularly at anyone. It's not real! she thought. She glanced around at dragons and gorillas, all ferocious, but engaged in the same mechanical actions.

Then she noticed the row of neat blue signs on the right-hand side:

- PIN THE PTAIL ON THE PTERODACTYL
- ARTBREAK ARCADE
- MONSTER MUSEUM
- BUILD YOUR OWN BOT

"Where did you find this place, Lulu?"

"Rrrrrr." The little Chihuahua leaped out of her arms and started after an enormous blue chicken.

"Hey, come back!" Sylvie managed to grab Lulu, but tripped over the "Monster Museum" sign. There was a click, and an instant later she and Lulu were in a dim gallery, surrounded by the strangest-looking creatures Sylvie had ever seen. A blob with dozens of eyes trembled on one platform, each eye turning in a different direction. An alligator with a woman's body, her shapely legs dangling, perched on the edge of the next platform. Then came a stegosaurus with a giant bee stinger for a tail. All looked disturbingly alive, although Sylvie could see that they were just exhibits.

There were signs beneath each platform telling what each one was. A platform on the right caught her attention because she could see nothing on it whatever. Coming closer, she detected a tiny brown mouse with a spot of yellow on the tip of its tail. SHAPE SHIFTER, said the placard beneath it. That certainly didn't seem very scary. Sylvie was just turning away when she heard a loud hiss and saw the mouse swell up and extend till it became a huge writhing eel with six little feet, on each of which were three toes with tiny yellow toenails.

Sylvie looked around her, holding the dog tightly. "Let's get out of here, Lulu," she whispered and stepped on the sign, HOME PAGE. Instantly they were back where they'd started, with the feathered rhino and giant chicken. "I'm going to get you home!"

They stepped through the rectangular panel and were out in the corridor.

Thank You
for Stopping By.
Have a Nice Day!

"You don't want that cookie, Lulu." The dog was sniffing the glowing disk.

Suddenly, from up ahead came the reverberation of an enormous roar. It echoed from wall to wall, corridor to corridor. "It's him!" whispered Sylvie, clutching the little dog and moving towards the sound. Another roar, louder now, rebounded past them. Lulu began to whimper.

On they flew, the roars becoming angrier as they went. Lulu was now whimpering continually. Then she lifted up her head and let out a howl. "Ow-owwwww-ooo!"

The roaring stopped at once.

"Lulu! Be quiet! He knows we're here!"

But Lulu was a little brown-and-white bundle of fear. "Ow-owooooo!"

"Stop it!"

Sylvie stopped by an illuminated panel, opened it with a touch of her hand, and shoved Lulu inside.

"Stay there. I'll be back for you."

> Thank You
> for Stopping By.
> Have a Nice Day!

She hurried on, but the labyrinth had fallen silent. At the end of a corridor she paused, then crept forwards.

Around the next turn she came upon a red panel, much like others she'd seen, except this firewall looked thicker and was reinforced with brass locks and fittings. Electricity shimmered across its surface, and the silence seemed to deepen.

She floated up to it and stopped, trying to make no sound. The red-tinged glass revealed nothing, but she was sure she had found the right place. Come on, she thought. Let me see you!

A momentary darkness passed over the glass, then disappeared. Something was in there. The shadow again appeared – the vague outline of an enormous head. A low rasping sound came through the door. The creature's breathing!

Sylvie fumbled with her locket, her fingers clumsy. It opened, and she gasped. The head of a dragonlike creature was staring out at her. Whenever the shadow moved behind the red door, the monster moved inside the locket, its yellow eyes glinting. It was like having a peephole into the creature's lair.

Sylvie looked straight at the shadow behind the door.

"My name," she said in a clear strong voice, "is Princess Sylvie, from King Walther's kingdom, in the book known as *The Great Good Thing*."

The shadowy head cocked to one side.

"You can hear me," she continued, consciously projecting her voice from her belly, the way Rosetta had taught her. "So listen. I am going to stop you, do you understand? *I'm going to stop you!*"

She saw the shadowy head rear back, and suddenly the loudest sound she had ever heard knocked her against the opposite wall. She was dazed and began to fear that, firewall or not, the beast would come crashing through.

Not waiting a moment, she flew down the hallway the way she'd come. She glanced back to see if the beast had followed. It was making a huge commotion, battering itself against the firewall, but had not broken it. She whisked on.

Lulu! she thought, trying to get her bearings. Where did I leave her?

Ahead stretched an irregular row of glowing disks. Must be around here! She wished she had paid more attention to where she'd put Lulu. She began opening any door that had a cookie in front of it. Antique candlesticks, maps of the New York subway system, wine-making machines, but no Lulu.

"Here, girl!" she called.

From several corridors behind, she heard a tremendous splintering sound and then a roar, louder than before. The creature was free!

Crashing and banging echoed through the corridors behind her as she raced on. Suddenly, a different sound, like a blast of air from a furnace, reached her, and the corridor grew warm, then hot. Sylvie glanced back. The monster appeared round the corner, its leathery hide gleaming in the dim light and its head wreathed in smoke. Seeing Sylvie, it opened its huge jaws and shot out a jet of flame.

Left! Sylvie thought, and veered down another hallway just before the flames reached her, sizzling the wall.

Desperate to put as many partitions as possible between herself and the beast, she took a right turn, then a quick left and another left, only to find herself at a dead end. There was no way forwards!

Back! She flew the way she'd come, then zoomed to the right at the next corner. The whole maze was heating up, the walls warm to the touch. The creature seemed to be gaining on her. It knew this place intimately, Sylvie thought. Certainly it had no trouble following her.

She came to a crossroads and opened her locket for guidance. Pointing it to the left, she saw what looked like converging walls – another dead end. Quickly she pointed the locket to the right – more walls coming together. Either way was a trap! The beast must have *chased* her this way. It was anticipating her moves before she knew what they were herself!

Desperate, Princess Sylvie pointed the locket along the hall she had just come down. She was amazed to see the labyrinth opening into empty space.

"But I just came from there!" she said aloud. Who said this locket worked as a compass anyway? You never knew what would show up! Sometimes it was an image from the past, at other times the future. Still . . .

She quickly pointed the locket in the three directions again, and the same images appeared. A voice from far inside her whispered: Trust it. Trust the path.

Sylvie shut the locket and hurried back the way she had come. If she died, she would die trusting the one who had created her and the path that had led her to this moment. Nonetheless, she couldn't help feeling doubts when she felt the passage growing hotter and hotter.

Her cheeks flushed, she gritted her teeth and pushed on, her fear increasing as she went. Turning a corner, she found herself at the start of a long corridor. There at the other end, gnashing and slavering, stood the fiery beast she had been fleeing. It saw her and gave a roar of surprise. Then it shook its massive head and reared up on its hind legs, its jaws opening to let loose a fatal stream of flame.

Suddenly stars were everywhere – nothing but stars and bright meteors zooming towards Sylvie's head, and then veering away at the last moment. No hallway, no monster, only galaxies upon galaxies.

Screensaver! Sylvie remembered, flying straight ahead towards the place where the beast had last stood. Hind legs, she remembered, ducking her head and flying so low she felt her shoes skimming the ground. The heat increased suddenly and she heard a great furnace blast from somewhere overhead, although she could see nothing but stars on all sides.

Then coolness struck her forehead and she knew she had passed beneath the creature and was on the other side. She couldn't see where she was flying and scraped painfully against the left-hand wall.

At once, the screensaver disappeared, and Sylvie was astonished to see the end of the maze looming ahead, the corridor leading out into space – cyberspace this time, space without any stars at all.

Chapter Twelve

The journey home took place in a kind of dream. With nothing to measure her progress by, the darkness felt endless. Finally a small bright shape appeared in the distance, then several others. They grew larger as she approached. By the jagged outline of one of them, she recognized The Great Deletion.

Grabbing its edge and pulling herself up into the story, Sylvie suddenly felt someone's hands helping to lift her. Laurel had been waiting there the whole time!

"Thank God!" whispered the girl with the dark blue eyes.

Sylvie felt an unexpected surge of emotion as she hugged her friend. Her eyes blurred with tears.

"What is it? What happened?" said Laurel.

At first, Sylvie's throat was so tight she could manage only one word: *"Awful!"*

"Take your time. Let's walk a bit."

Sylvie took a big breath and puffed it out in a sigh. "I'm all right." As they set off down the castle corridor she began describing the creature she had seen.

Laurel stopped her. "Why not wait and tell your parents about it? They need to know."

Sylvie nodded. "All right."

The king and queen, who hadn't realised Sylvie had left the kingdom, were astonished to hear about her journey into the maze where the monster lived. Her description of the creature upset them deeply; and the thought that her little dog was still in there brought the queen to tears.

"I'll get her out next time," Sylvie promised.

King Walther raised his heavy brows in alarm. "No, you won't! You were almost killed!"

"I'm not saying I would go alone."

"We have our knights. We can raise an army!"

"I wasn't thinking of an army exactly."

"Knights slay dragons. It's part of their training," he said.

"Father, we have never had a dragon in our kingdom. Our knights would be helpless."

"And you were not?"

"Sire," ventured the girl with the dark blue eyes, who had been quiet until now, "perhaps you should meet with your councillors. Let them share their wisdom. I'm sure they will have a plan to suggest."

"An excellent idea, as always."

"You'll let us know what you decide?"

"I will, certainly, my dear."

Leaving the throne room, the girls passed Pingree. "I see you took some heat from your father," he remarked, his eyebrows dancing.

"What do you mean, you nonsensical creature?" Sylvie said.

"I mean your dress got scorched."

Sylvie hadn't noticed, but there were burn marks on her sleeve and hem. "Just dirt," she said, hurrying on.

"We'll see who makes sense," Pingree called after her in his reedy voice, "and who makes nonsense!"

Crossing the drawbridge, Sylvie stopped to look down at the lilies covering the surface of the moat. "What was it you were telling my father?" she said, turning to Laurel. "'Meet with your councillors'?"

Laurel smiled slightly. "That will keep them busy."

Sylvie's eyes brightened.

"You know it will take them days to agree on anything," the girl continued. "That gives us some time. Can you find Mr Fangl and meet me by the big hemlock where we were before?"

Sylvie set off at a run. "Thank you!" she called over her shoulder.

A short time later, Princess Sylvie and Fangl were taking the footpath into the forest. They passed a stand of yew trees with their poisonous scarlet berries, and then ducked under the low-hanging boughs of the hemlock. There they found Laurel and, to Sylvie's surprise, Prince Godric.

"Where are you tuh-taking us?" said Godric, eyeing Sylvie nervously.

"I think we need to meet with Miss Stein," said Laurel.

"The outlaw?"

Laurel smiled. "The outlaw, yes." She jumped onto the scroll bar on the side of the screen. "Everybody ready?" She rose upwards, climbed over the little pictures along the top, and punched a button, throwing them all into Rosetta's hiding place.

As Sylvie and the others suddenly disappeared, a small, spindle-legged man stared up through the thick leaves of a rhododendron. He shook his head and eyed the scroll bar doubtfully. What did that girl do? he thought. Went to the top, climbed over there, and . . . He pulled on his chin.

"The king will be interested in this!" he said aloud. Pingree started back towards the castle, giggling. "Very interested!"

He was just leaving the footpath for the castle road when he ran into the reeve and a young squire. They were standing beside a woodcutter's cottage, which had sunk partway into the ground.

"Another soft spot," explained the reeve when Pingree asked. "The poor fellow barely got out in time."

"Well, I've got something more interesting to show you than soggy sod!" said the jester, puffing out his little chest.

The reeve, a man with steely hair and a keen eye, knew Pingree well and didn't like him. He'd been the victim of too many practical jokes. "Oh yes?" he said.

"You want to capture that outlaw woman, don't you?"

"You know where she is?" said the squire.

"That would be quite a plume in your helmets,

wouldn't it?" said Pingree, looking from one to the other.

"Speak up, you squealing little git!" growled the reeve. "If you know where she is, tell us!"

"What will you give me if I do?"

"I'll let you live another day."

Pingree considered this. He also considered the intensity of the men's impatience and the depth of the furrows in their frowns. "I accept your offer!" Prancing with self-satisfaction, he led the men into the forest.

The shepherdess stood up to meet her visitors. "Hello, Prince," she said, giving a curtsy to Godric. "Mr Fangl, everybody. Sylvie, you're back!" She started towards her, but stopped, taking in the burn marks and the soot on her forehead. "What happened?"

Laurel gave the princess a little nod. "Tell them."

Sylvie settled herself, leaning against the white background, and told about her adventures in the labyrinth. Prince Godric seemed on the verge of interrupting several times, but held back. Fangl stared intently at the ground, as if understanding were to be found in its blank surface.

When she had finished, Fangl cleared his throat. "Excuse me, Your Highness," he said, "but did you say, 'bot'?"

"What?"

"Not 'what'. *'Bot.'* You were describing the signs in that person's game arcade. I thought you said, 'Build your own bot.'"

"Yes."

"Could that mean 'robot'?"

Sylvie shrugged. "What's that?"

"Ah," said the geometry teacher, "I keep forgetting you live in the Middle Ages. A robot is a machine that works automatically or by remote control. It can look like anything: a man, an animal . . ."

"Even a monster," Rose put in, her eyebrow rising.

"Yes, but it's not real," Fangl said. "Not alive, I mean."

Sylvie gave her head a little shake. "Well, the monster I ran into was alive enough."

"True. It's just that the kind of creature you described doesn't exist."

"Look at these burn marks. Do they exist?"

He nodded. "An excellent point, Your Highness."

Prince Godric gave a toss of his magnificent head of hair. "I am thinking," he said, "of my other self. He can be a bit of a monster, too; but he's confined to his cave. Is there any way we can — if we can't kill the beast — confine him in some way?"

Sylvie looked at the prince with surprise. He wasn't stuttering! Evidently, Rosetta's classes had done a lot for him. He even had a brain in that pretty head of his! "What a good idea, Godric," she said.

Godric blushed.

"We'd need a cage," Fangl said, picking up the thought. "One that no creature can break out of."

"It would have to be made of unbreakable materials," said Sylvie, remembering how the monster had crashed through the firewall.

"And it would have to be a perfect shape," Laurel added, giving Sylvie a significant look.

"Yes!" the princess said, pride filling her voice. "Well, we know what the perfect shape is. Professor Fangl has created it!"

Fangl looked alarmed. "Oh, no, no. That's just a little experiment I was trying out. Of no importance, no importance at all."

"That's not what you told *me*."

"No, no." The geometry teacher seemed almost to be pleading. "You promised you wouldn't say anything."

Sylvie stopped herself. "I'm sorry," she said. "I didn't mean to upset you. It just seemed . . ."

"Really, it's nothing."

"Professor," said Godric, "if you know something that can help us, I think you really ought to tell us what it is."

Fangl looked from one face to the other.

"Do you want to keep this discovery to yourself?" said Laurel gently.

"No, of course not. It's just . . ." He faltered. "It's just that I never discovered anything before. It should be . . ."

"Written up in an article?" Laurel said.

"Well, yes."

"Unveiled at a symposium?"

"You embarrass me, but yes."

"If you were alive," the girl continued, "all these things would most certainly happen. Regrettably, however . . ."

"I know," he said in a subdued voice.

"So I'm afraid that all you can do with your great new invention is save your friends."

Fangl hung his head. "You're right, of course."

"So then," said Prince Godric, "tell us about this shape. If you will," he added.

The teacher gave another look around at the others, and then nodded. "All of you will be my symposium," he said. "You'll be my article in *Geometrician's Quarterly*." He paused, still hesitating. "Very well," he said and cleared his throat. He began describing what the Paragon looked like, but he used too many words no one had ever heard before.

"*Show* us," Princess Sylvie interrupted. "Can you draw on this white wall?"

"I think so." Fangl rummaged in his jacket pocket and pulled out a piece of blue chalk. Quickly he sketched a square, and from that base he sent lines slanting upwards into equilateral triangles and further squares. "The challenge," he said, "is to make a curve using only straight lines." His blue chalk scraped line after line on the wall. In another moment, the lines were all in place and the three-dimensional illusion complete. The result was almost spherical. There was something simple about it, inevitable, and quite beautiful. When they saw it before them, everyone burst into applause.

"Ah!" cried Rosetta with pleasure.

"But can we build it?" said Godric. "And out of what?"

Fangl shook his head.

"Miss Stein?" said Laurel.

Rosetta looked up.

Laurel raised her eyebrow a fraction but said nothing more.

"What? How would *I* build this shape? Obviously, if you were going deep into cyberspace, you couldn't bring anything with you. You'd just have yourselves, and . . ." She stopped abruptly. Her hand went to her mouth.

"What are you thinking?" said Laurel.

"But they're not trained. They couldn't."

"How long would it take to train them?"

"It depends."

Sylvie set her hands on her hips. "What are you two *talking* about?"

Rosetta turned to Sylvie. "Laurel thinks I can train you all in energy projection."

"I didn't say a word," Laurel said, smiling.

Godric spoke. "You mean the lines of energy you were teaching us to send out?"

"We were only able to maintain that for a few moments," said Sylvie, remembering the elation she'd felt when she first succeeded in projecting a thin beam of blue light from the centre of her body.

"Those lines seemed pretty fragile. Could we build something this complex?" said Godric.

"And maintain it?" Fangl added.

Rosetta shook her head. "It would take a lot of work."

"We could meet in here at night," said Sylvie.

They looked at one another: the Author, the geometrician, the yogi, the prince and the heroine. The agreement was sealed.

"Here it is!" Pingree stood beneath the hemlock, gesturing upwards.

"Here is what?"

"You mean you don't see her? We must do something about your eyes, Sir Reeve."

"If you don't answer me, I'll nail you up by your ears!"

"What a way to talk! All right, gentlemen, if you'll kindly step this way." He ducked under the hemlock branch and held it. "Watch your heads."

Pingree had been looking back at the men and didn't notice the soggy spot just ahead. "Yiii!" he cried out as he sank into it to his knees. Naturally, he let go of the hemlock branch, which thwacked the reeve across the face.

"That's it!" the man yelled. He looked around. "Where is that fool?"

"Probably hiding," said the squire, coming through behind.

"Pingree, get over here!" the reeve bellowed. "It'll go worse for you, if you don't."

There was no sound but wind moving through the top branches of the hemlock. The two men looked at each other.

"Strange business," mused the reeve.

"It is that," said the squire.

"Houses sinking, people disappearing, animals changing colour . . ."

"Animals, sir?"

The reeve gave a nod at a piglet poking its wet little nose out from under the rhododendron bush. The pig was bright green.

Chapter Thirteen

*E*ight days later, five friends met at dawn by the edge of a great empty place in the story. It wasn't the torn section known as The Great Deletion. That place was inside the castle and well guarded these days. But the terrible deletions had continued during the week, and there were now several large rips in the story. This one was by the road to Humped Mountain.

The friends had undergone secret training sessions, after midnight and before dawn, till their bodies were sore and their minds bleary from the effort of concentration. They themselves would admit that they did not feel ready. Only two days earlier they had succeeded for the first time in constructing the Paragon, using lines of energy projected from the centre of their bodies and connecting with the bodies of the others. It was a triumphant moment, but they were unable to maintain the shape for more than a few seconds before the lines wobbled and veered apart.

Now time had run out. The king had finished his consultations and called up thirty of his most trusted knights. They were drilled on the techniques of dragon slaying (a subject many of the men remembered only dimly) and were preparing to set out the next day. When they weren't bragging or clanking about the courtyard practising war manoeuvres, the knights were sharpening their swords, polishing their shields and burnishing their breastplates. Sylvie shook her head. With all that equipment they wouldn't stand a chance.

Not that she held much hope for Godric, Rosetta, Laurel and herself. They were the ones who would make the trip. Fangl felt he was too old to battle with monsters. Probably he had always been too old. And his attempts to send out beams of energy from his stomach were not a success. His contributions had been providing the shape of the cage and helping work out the plans. The idea was to use what he called the "least necessary" principle. That meant travelling light and

bringing no weapons. They carried within them everything they needed. When their minds were joined and
their concentration pure, they drew on an energy that
nothing could break.

"Are we ready then?" Laurel said.

Sylvie went to Fangl and gave him a gentle hug, then
joined hands with the others in a circle.

"Godspeed, children," said Fangl.

Laurel gripped Sylvie's hand on one side and Rose's
on the other. Godric took his place beside Rosetta.

"On three?" said Sylvie. "One, two . . ."

They jumped and were immediately submerged in
blackness. Sylvie shot a glance behind her and saw
Fangl peering down from the bright world of the
book. Then he was gone.

"I don't think I like this!" It was Godric's voice.

"Don't worry," Sylvie said. "The darkness isn't
forever."

"Are we moving?" said Rosetta. "I don't feel any
wind."

"There isn't any wind. We're not outside. We're
inside."

No one spoke for a long time. It reassured Sylvie to have
Laurel beside her. If she had to move through darkness, it

was good to know that the Author was holding her hand. And yet it was Sylvie, not Laurel, who was the guide in this strange world.

After a time that seemed both endless and no time at all, a distant light struggled towards them through folds of darkness.

"The labyrinth!" Sylvie called out. "Remember the plan: single file!"

Willing herself to go faster, Sylvie moved out in front, with Laurel, Rosetta and Godric following, still holding hands.

Soon the maze loomed before them. "Let's slow down here," Sylvie said.

As rehearsed, everyone silently concentrated on the word "slower". They slipped easily through the entranceway and glided down gloomy corridors. Sylvie was relieved to see that the cookies had remained on their little plastic trays outside the glow-ing panels. She signalled the others to stop.

"Okay," she whispered. "We're not going to talk from here on, so if you have any questions, ask them now."

They all looked at one another.

"How far," whispered Godric, "before we get to the lair?"

"Quite a way. We'll be following the cookies."

Godric nodded.

"Now you all know how to propel yourselves," said Sylvie. "So we don't need to hold hands any more. Any other questions?"

"Yeah," said Rosetta, "how do I get to Croton Falls?"

Sylvie shot her a quick smile. "Anything else?"

When no one spoke, Sylvie moved ahead, the others following separately. The first thing Godric did was bump face first into the wall, but soon he got the knack of steering. When Sylvie turned down a corridor and saw no cookies up ahead, she hand-signalled the others and doubled back. Soon they came to a crossroads. Seeing no glowing disks in any direction, Sylvie clicked open the locket, hoping for a clue, but was disappointed to see nothing but a small mouse with a touch of yellow on its tail.

The next turn to the left looked familiar to Sylvie, even though there were no cookies out. She remembered that last time she had simply floated down several corridors without opening any panels.

"Come on," she whispered, moving through the greyish light.

Two turns later, she was rewarded by the sight of a

row of little round disks. They were on course, after all.

Rosetta drifted up beside Sylvie. "I feel something," she whispered.

Sylvie nodded and put her finger to her lips. There had been no sound, but she sensed they were close. The four friends turned another corner. Suddenly, there it was – a red firewall halfway down on the left. They floated over to it and came to a stop.

Something was different. The wall was intact (it must have been repaired since last time), but there was no rippling of electricity across the surface. The red-tinted glass looked dull, without any illumination or shadows moving behind it. The place, in fact, seemed deserted.

Sylvie and Laurel exchanged looks. Sylvie checked the locket, but it gave back no image. Was it possible the beast had moved to another section of the labyrinth? Gathering her courage, Sylvie reached out and touched the red panel.

No electric shock, no ear-shattering roar, nothing. The door sprang open. Sylvie gave a toss of her head to signal the others to follow.

The place was a ruin: a wooden table slumping in the

corner, chairs splintered, even the floorboards split and pitted. If Sylvie had not seen the monstrous creature that lived there, she would have thought the room had suffered an explosion.

Then she noticed a vague glow coming from an adjoining room. She signalled the others to be quiet. This could easily be a trap. It had occurred to her, in fact, that getting here had been entirely too easy. Still, there was no way to go now but forwards. She crept to the entrance and peered into the next room.

"My God!" she whispered.

"What is it?" breathed Rosetta.

Laurel took hold of Sylvie's arm.

The room was huge, a dilapidated but once-impressive auditorium, with rows of wooden theatre seats stretching back into darkness. In the centre was a large bare area, like a stage, a spotlight beaming down through the dusty air and revealing the creature that stood waiting for them.

It was far from the beast Sylvie had expected, but it shocked her more than any fire-breathing monster could have. Standing before them, slightly stoop-shouldered, the spotlight bouncing off his bald spot while he held his dented hat in his hands, was Norbert Fangl.

Chapter Fourteen

A dozen thoughts raced through Sylvie's mind as she stood gaping, each thought more senseless than the last. Fangl is the monster?

Impossible.

Fangl is *controlling* the monster?

Fangl masterminded the attacks on the story?

Ridiculous.

Fangl's being held prisoner? A hostage? That, yes, was a possibility.

"Is it you, Fangl?" Sylvie called.

The skinny geometry teacher raised his eyes. Seeing her, he gave a little wave.

"Are you all right?" Sylvie called out.

He smiled his sad little smile but didn't reply.

"Be careful," Godric whispered to Sylvie.

"Careful of Fangl?"

Under the spotlight, the old tutor started to feel in his trouser pocket, then his jacket pocket and finally his shirt pocket. He appeared to pull something out, something invisible from where Sylvie and the others stood, and held it in his cupped hand. He gestured for them to come and see.

"What do you have there?" called Sylvie.

Fangl merely continued to gesture, beckoning her closer.

Laurel held Sylvie's arm. "I wouldn't," she said.

"It's Fangl!" Sylvie protested. "He wants to show us something." She broke away and started to cross the cavernous room towards the spotlit stage.

"Princess!" Godric called, starting after her.

She waved him back and went on. Yes, she thought, coming closer, as unbelievable as it might seem, her old tutor had arrived before they had. He'd said he wasn't coming, but maybe he changed his mind. Maybe he thought of something, or found something that would help them. But why didn't he speak?

Sylvie was only ten feet from her teacher when she paused. There did seem something different about him. She looked him over carefully. Same skinny shoulders, same bald spot, same kindly eyes. Her eyes travelled down. Yes, there were the same wrinkled shirt and rumpled jacket. Same old corduroy trousers and brown shoes with, strangely enough . . .

Sylvie gasped.

She forced a smile, trying not to show alarm. "Oh, wait, Fangl! I have something for you, too. Let me just get it."

She backed away till she reached the others. "Take your positions right now," she muttered through smiling teeth. "Hurry!"

Her companions broke free of their stunned immobility and fanned out around the high-ceilinged chamber. Laurel was opposite Sylvie; Godric opposite Rosetta.

Rosetta's voice intoned: "Close your eyes, everyone. Drop into your centre."

Sylvie tried to force Fangl out of her thoughts and settle her consciousness into her body. At first, she was aware of nothing but her own talking mind telling her how crazy it was to close her eyes when there was danger before her. If only she could maintain her concentration! But she was good at throwing herself into a role and soon was able to sink deeper.

The figure of Norbert Fangl seemed confused. He

looked from one to the other and continued to beckon to them.

"We find our centre," said Rosetta, her hair flowing out with a life of its own, "and from this depth we can feel ourselves connected, belly to belly. From here we draw our strength, like the roots of giant redwoods that interlock beneath the earth."

Sylvie felt a growing awareness of her core. Warmth began to flow through her.

"Because we are so grounded," chanted Rosetta, "we extend ourselves and go beyond what we thought we were."

A sensation of uncoiling power began moving upwards in Sylvie; she could feel it building.

"Sylvie is bridging her energy to Godric in a clear line."

Sylvie's body began to tremble as a rush of energy swept through her. She heard Rosetta's chanting voice, sounding distant, and opened her eyes to see a shimmering blue thread extended from her own stomach to the corresponding power centre in Godric. She felt a bubble of joy at her success, but quickly dismissed it and continued to concentrate on sending out energy.

"We are increasing that flow of power *now*."

The line grew thicker and brighter.

"Now Godric is extending his power to Laurel."

A hesitant line wobbled in the air a moment, then flickered out. Godric closed his eyes, frowning with concentration. Soon a new line of electricity made a crooked line. He relaxed his brow, letting the force beam out of him. The line began to straighten, like a thread pulled taut. Once Godric's line was established, Laurel directed her energy to Rosetta, who in turn sent a strong line to Sylvie.

They had created a glowing square around the edge of the room! They could hear it humming!

The figure of Norbert Fangl seemed not to understand what was happening. He took off his hat and put it on again, gesturing to each person in turn. Still he did not speak.

"We are maintaining our connection, belly to belly," Rosetta's voice chanted. "From this place we now extend a second line upwards."

As they had practised, Sylvie beamed her line of energy to meet Godric's at the midpoint above their heads. A glowing triangle appeared.

Norbert Fangl was becoming frantic. He mashed his hat

in his hands, put it on, reached into his pockets, beckoned. There was something mechanical in his repeated actions, but no one had time to look at him. Godric extended another upward line, meeting Laurel's. Then Laurel and Rosetta created a triangle. Soon four triangles trembled in the air.

That was when Fangl began changing shape, his eyes growing round, his cheeks sinking into hairy jowls, his nose flattening and blackening until he had transmogrified into a huge bulldog with a corkscrew tail. The beast growled, baring bright yellow fangs.

"Keep your eyes closed and your focus clear!" Rosetta called out.

Sylvie knew this was the most difficult part. From the peaks of the triangles, the four friends would have to bend their lines of energy to create an upside-down triangle on top of the lower triangle. Complete concentration was essential.

The great black dog began racing about within the lines of energy. It tried to jump over the lowest line, but was knocked back by a powerful electric shock. It couldn't get out!

The Paragon was almost complete. All that remained was connecting the upper triangles, high overhead.

"Deeper, now," chanted Rosetta. "We feel the lines of our energy sourced in the cave, burning brightly. We breathe into that fire and prepare to extend the final line . . ."

"RRRRH!"

Sylvie opened her eyes to see the bulldog swelling unrecognisably, turning into an enormous scaly beast with a thrashing tail and yellow eyes. It was the monster Sylvie had confronted before! Despite her efforts, she felt her concentration falter, and then her lines of energy veered off at a crazy angle.

Godric's construction had already fallen apart.

"Close your eyes," cried Rosetta, whose own lines of energy were shaking badly. "We return to the centre for strength. There is safety in the cave."

"RRAAARGH!" The beast whipped around, brandishing its powerful reptilian tail. Its slit eyes shifted from one to the other, choosing its target. The animal's talons raked the wooden platform, tearing out great splinters.

Then a tiny wisp of smoke curled from the side of its mouth. "Get down! Down! Down!" Sylvie yelled and immediately dived behind a row of seats just as a stream of fire sailed over her head.

"Rebuild! Rebuild!" she shouted, bobbing up again from behind the next row of seats.

"Take your positions!" Rosetta cried, drawing courage from Sylvie.

Godric's face was pale, but he closed his eyes to concentrate. Immediately, the beast wheeled around, its rigid tail catching the prince on his head and knocking him off his feet. He lay senseless, his forehead bleeding freely.

"My God!" cried Rosetta, starting towards him.

"No!" warned Laurel. "We have to build the Paragon."

"But Godric . . ." There was a quaver in Rosetta's voice. Her hair seemed to be hiding behind her. "Don't we need four points?"

"We can do it with three!" Sylvie called out. "We'll start with the triangle!"

"But he's hurt!"

"We need your strength, Rose," Sylvie called out. "We need it here!"

The beast was turning about slowly, not sure which of the remaining three it should destroy next.

"We are dropping down inside," Sylvie called out, willing herself to close her eyes despite the creature before her. "We are rooting deep into our centre of power."

Sylvie had never led this exercise before, but with Rosetta wavering, there was no choice.

"We feel the power building," Sylvie chanted. She began to feel a warmth in her stomach. "I am extending my line of energy to Laurel, my Author, my dear creator." It felt good to say that, and even better when a thin electric stream sailed out like a blue fishing line and reached the centre of Laurel's body. Although Sylvie had done the extending, it was clear that the energy was flowing both ways, because suddenly she felt herself a part of Laurel's mind, just as Laurel was a part of hers.

Then Laurel threw her line to Rosetta, who was still trembling. Rosetta's strength increased, and after several tries she was able to complete the circuit by connecting with Sylvie.

A triangle of blue light shimmered in the great hall. No time! Sylvie thought wildly. She forced her mind to push that thought aside.

"We will now extend two lines upwards from the core," she cried.

Moments later, six glowing lines reached up like searchlights.

"We're doing it!" cried Rosetta.

"Yes, we are," Sylvie called out. "You take it from here."

Rosetta resumed directing the exercise, coaching Laurel and Sylvie in how to bend the energy lines to create upright squares of light, then how to connect the final triangle on top of those squares.

With a soft snap of electricity, the Paragon was complete. The three young women suddenly felt more deeply connected than ever before, drawing power from one another as they stood at the base of this humming, circular, weblike marvel of a shape. Up close, it looked impossibly complex, but from a little distance it was simplicity itself. Sylvie felt a thrill of pleasure.

The beast, which had been watching in angry fascination, now focused on Sylvie, and opened its smoking maw.

There was no dodging this time, she knew. "I am anchored in the centre," she told herself, deep within her mind. "I *am* that power." She closed her eyes, and so heard rather than saw the violet flame jetting from the creature's mouth.

"RRAAAUUGH!"

Sylvie's eyes snapped open to see the monster

writing on the stage in pain. Then she realised: the flame it had hurled at her had rebounded and ravaged its own face!

Sylvie gave a laugh of triumph, but immediately felt the structure of the Paragon begin to quiver. Triumph had no place here, she realised. She began the chanting again, her eyes closed.

The trembling lessened.

With a deafening howl, the maddened creature let loose a new blast of flame. It zinged from one side of the Paragon to the other and rebounded instantly to the middle, where it engulfed the beast a second time.

Its screams were piteous as it raised itself on its haunches and pawed the air. A number of scales had blackened and broken off, flaking from its back. A glutinous fluid streamed from its eye sockets, and Sylvie realised with horror that the creature's eyeballs were melting. It was blind!

"Steady!" called Laurel.

"We find strength in the cave," Rosetta chanted.

In its agony, the great monster let loose one more blast of fire. This one hit one of the upper triangles, which sent it rebounding directly at the beast's head. With a strangled cry, the creature fell backwards, splintering the boards as it crashed to the ground, one leg twitching. In the intense heat, its skull split open, revealing a brain glowing like coals.

Sylvie felt such a mingling of revulsion and pity that she was unable to maintain her concentration. The others must have felt the same, because the lines of the Paragon came apart, sputtered and disappeared.

As they watched, a very strange thing happened. The monster began to contract, growing smaller until it resembled a black bulldog lying on its side, its tightly curled tail beginning to loosen and unwind. Then the animal grew thinner and longer, its hair replaced by human clothing.

"Oh!" Sylvie put her hand over her mouth at the sight of the dying Norbert Fangl.

But then, the shape of the old tutor began shrinking. It was no longer Fangl, no longer human. It became smaller and smaller, at last sprouting a few singed whiskers and turning into a mouse with a single yellow spot at the tip of its trembling tail.

Then the little animal turned transparent. Sylvie, Laurel and Rose bent closer, just as the creature disappeared entirely, replaced by a quick scroll of numbers and strange-looking letters hovering briefly in midair:

DêaCgreatgoodtŠ-´*ÿ°Âë$iß

f'''' êA„*mere*>*mirrr*}ÿ'ñlRY;

ât2 ——————óUMᵒ'g\8——

ã.Ùá⁻=)arroses4ßªÛVYÏD

ŸÈ·+$ŸeÒª¥Ëo

Œ/¹ÄÊi%*flea*/*tre*U‰oü

ù² ¿ ¿ ¿ ¿ ¿ ¿ ¿ ¿ ¿ ¿ ¿ ¿ ¿^

õøk I'Z2/fàà< ~ ~

Y'A`» 'bgunnÅx

@_{X>·<`frogers'àÆõl

 !¸KÄm†`ø

ìsAÆ/ ø . . . ——————————,

ÏfA°

Æ

Á

i

A moment later, with a soft pop, the numbers and letters disappeared, and the companions were alone in the dark chamber.

Chapter Fifteen

"Godric!" Rosetta cried. She ran to the prince, who lay beside a row of broken theatre seats. "Godric! Dear Godric!"

The other two ran to join her. There lay the handsome young man, with a pulsing wound on his forehead.

"Is he going to be all right?" Sylvie said.

Laurel touched her arm. Something in Laurel's eyes made Sylvie pause.

Rosetta was cradling the unconscious prince in her arms. "Wake," she whispered. "Wake, young prince." She looked at him with great tenderness; then she bent over him and gently kissed the wound on his forehead.

Godric's eyelids flickered slightly. He moaned and opened his eyes, gazing up at Rosetta.

"Wh-What?"

"Shh," Rosetta said. "Rest."

The young man smiled weakly. "Yes," he said, "maybe I will, just a minute. Thank you, dear Rosetta."

She tore a strip of material from the hem of her shepherdess dress and tied it around his wound.

Sylvie and Laurel exchanged a look. "'Dear Rosetta'?" whispered Sylvie.

Laurel raised an eyebrow. "Is that all right with you?"

For a moment Sylvie didn't know if it was or not. She was so used to being admired. Still . . . "You mean I won't have to fend off any more marriage proposals?"

Her friend with the dark blue eyes gave an expressive shrug.

Sylvie looked down and smiled. "Perfect," she murmured. She turned and walked around the dark room by herself. Her smile faded and she grew thoughtful, looking up at the cracked rafters, the dusty spotlight, the broken stage. She scanned the ceiling and rows of theatre seats extending into darkness.

What had just happened here? And those last figures

dancing like gnats in the air after the beast had disappeared – what were they?

A code.

Is that what it came down to? All that ferocity, that intelligence, that *intent*? Was it nothing more than a set of instructions?

Just then something caught her eye – a tiny point of light coming from the far wall. She made her way to it, climbing over a splintered seat. Strange, she thought, as she reached a small round hole and put her eye to it.

Sylvie found herself looking into a room with white curtains. It looked familiar somehow – a canopied bed, an ancient dark wood desk by a bay window. A lamp cast a yellow circle on a framed picture. She *did* know this place! The photograph – it was of Laurel as an old woman, with her children and grandchildren. This used to be her room – how long ago?

Sylvie's reverie was cut short when suddenly an angry-looking boy sat right in front of her, blocking her view. She heard a clacking sound and looked down and saw the keyboard of a computer. The boy was banging at it.

Oh my! she thought, looking back at his bespectacled face. Reflected in his round lenses she saw a computer screen bordered by small icons. Sylvie realised she was looking out through one of those icons right now.

For a moment she drew back from the peephole. Where, she thought, had she seen his face before? She put her eye back to the hole. The red hair, yes, and the pudgy cheeks and little eyes.

"Ricky!" she breathed. It was the boy who had burned their book decades ago. She was sure of it! "Laurel, come here!"

But her friend was helping Rosetta lift the prince to sitting position, and she didn't answer.

It couldn't be Ricky, of course. Laurel had told him that Claire's brother Ricky had died. But he'd had a son, she'd said. Yes, and the son had had a son, a boy just the age of this furious red-faced person before her.

"Work!" the boy cried out at the screen. "Where did you *go?*" He bashed the keys even harder than before, trying to make something appear. "Bring me my bot back!"

He reached over for a big sloppy jam sandwich and took a bite out of it. "This game's no good!"

In his agitation, a big gob of strawberry jam dropped onto the keyboard.

"Oh Riiiicky!" A distant female voice was calling.

"What?" he shouted towards the door.

"Your Aunt Lily's here. Please come down and say hello."

"Damn Aunt Lily!"

The boy reached for a paper napkin to wipe up the jam.

"Are you on your father's computer again?" came the woman's voice. "He told you not to use it any more, after . . ."

"Damn Father!"

"Are you on my computer?" boomed a heavy male voice. "You're no longer allowed to use it, son!"

A tall glass of chocolate milk was resting on the napkin. When the boy grabbed the napkin, the glass wobbled, then toppled onto the keyboard, sending sparks flying.

"My goodness!" whispered Sylvie, as the screen flickered.

The boy stood up in a rage, brought back his booted foot, and gave the computer a tremendous kick. The peephole went black.

Sylvie flinched away, her hands on her cheeks.

There was silence.

"What is it?" called Laurel, looking over at her.

Sylvie walked slowly to the others. Godric looked shaky, but he was standing, and Rosetta was encouraging him to lean on her.

"You saw something," said Laurel, noticing Sylvie's frown.

"I did," Sylvie replied. She gave her friend a long look. "You've got quite a family, haven't you?"

"Ricky?" Laurel said softly.

Sylvie nodded. A smile started across her lips. "On the bright side, I think that we won't have any more troubles with our story."

As they set off for home, they all called out for Lulu, their voices ringing along the corridor. Sylvie was sure the dog couldn't be far away. Still, it had been over a week since Sylvie had thrust it into one of these doorways. Had anyone fed the poor animal?

They were lucky. In the next hallway, they heard a muffled barking. Faint sounds of trumpets and piccolos came through a panel on the right. Sylvie touched the door and it opened to the crash of a cymbal. Majorettes marched by while a bare-chested man swooped past on a trapeze. And there, atop a red bass drum, was Lulu. She was doing back flips!

Catching sight of Princess Sylvie, the little Chihuahua scampered over and leaped into her arms, turning around and nuzzling and squealing.

A clown came up to them. "You no taking Schweppski?" he said. "We are needing her for our big ect."

"Your ect? No, no, we have to take her," Sylvie said with a smile. "But thanks for looking after her so well."

"She is big tellent, dot dog. You see the fleeps?"

"The flips? Yes. Wonderful!"

Sylvie managed to get the squirming dog out into the hallway, and after much waving and kazoo-tooting, the panel closed. "Well, Lulu," she said. "I see you've been having quite a time!"

At last they reached the kingdom, though at first they didn't recognise the hole they had used. The opening was so much narrower than before. They just had room to squeeze through. Lulu was the first, and she immediately started doing back flips while the others clambered up. When they were all safely on their feet, they found someone there to greet them. Sylvie rushed into his arms.

"Fangl!" she cried. "I was so worried about you!"

"About me, princess? But I didn't even go!"

"I know, I know. Thank God!"

The old geometry teacher looked helplessly over at Laurel.

"First," said the girl with the dark blue eyes, "let me say that your marvellous Paragon worked perfectly."

Fangl's eyes lit up, and his smile went wider than anyone in the book had ever seen it. "Did it really? It *worked?*"

"Oh yes!" Sylvie broke in. "That monster couldn't get out at all!"

"Between your ingenious shape, sir," said Godric, "and Miss Stein's remarkable energy lines . . ."

"It's everybody's energy," said Rosetta. "I did nothing. I lost my focus."

"Miss Stein," said the prince, "I lost *consciousness.*"

Fangl held up his hands. "Why doesn't somebody start at the beginning?"

So Laurel, who was calmest, gave a quick sketch of what had happened in the maze.

The tutor looked confused. "But how did you know I wasn't really the one you were seeing?"

"I knew something was different," said Sylvie in her quick voice, "but I couldn't tell what – until I noticed the socks."

"Socks, Princess?"

"You often wear a wrinkled shirt, Fangl, I'm sorry to tell you. And rumpled trousers. You seldom have on a matching tie. But you would never, ever, *ever* put on yellow socks!"

Fangl laughed. "Who *would*?"

"A shape-shifting bot, that's who. Every time it changed form, it always had a touch of bright yellow somewhere."

Fangl looked down at Lulu, who had now begun doing *forward* flips. "What has happened to this poor animal?"

"This poor animal has joined the circus."

"Well, the queen will be ecstatic to see her."

"Yes!" Sylvie said. "We need to get to the castle right away."

Rosetta was looking down along the road. "I have the feeling the castle is coming to *us*."

Sure enough, a band of knights was marching smartly in their direction, dust rising in the air behind them and sunlight glancing from their shields. Leading them was King Walther on an armoured horse. He reined in before his daughter, raising a new cloud of dust.

"Sylvie," he said, coughing and waving his arms, "where have you been?"

"We've been having a little adventure."

"Very nice, but you should have told us. Is Pingree with you?"

"I haven't seen him."

"He's been missing since yesterday." The king suddenly caught sight of Rosetta. "Lord Vaux!" he barked. "Arrest that woman!"

"Father, no!"

"Don't defend her, after what she has done."

The knight named Vaux stepped forwards and seized Rosetta roughly by the arm.

"After what Rose has done," declared Sylvie in a stony voice, "we should all be on our knees thanking her!"

"I have no time to discuss it. We're off on an expedition."

"May I ask where you're going?"

The king lowered his voice confidentially. "You needn't tell the others, but we're going to slay the monster in the maze."

"Are you really?" Sylvie whispered back. "And are you going to ride your horse into this deletion?"

"Child, I don't think you need to bother your head about military strategy."

"You're right, Father. It's only that your big old horse may not fit."

"What!" He looked over at the opening, which was becoming increasingly smaller. Now not even Lulu could have squeezed through it.

"It seems to be *healing*," Sylvie said. "Look around. Do you see that wordpool over there? It's drying up!"

"How is this possible?"

"I don't know. But I don't think we'll find Ben Gunn around here, either."

"What's going on, daughter?"

Sylvie was smiling broadly now. "Maybe something happened while we were in there rescuing Lulu and slaying the monster."

"Slaying . . ." King Walther stared at his daughter and then at Lulu, who had begun growling at the horse's foreleg.

"You mean . . . the battle's over?"

"It is."

"The field is won?"

"Complete victory!"

"And you did this?"

"We all did. It took every one of us. Especially Rosetta."

The king shook his head in wonderment. He looked back over his knights, many of whom had been listening hard. "Well," he said, "it appears that our mission has changed somewhat."

Still mounted, he called his lieutenant over for a whispered consultation. In the midst of it, he turned again to Sylvie. "Are you *sure* about Miss Stein? She helped you?"

"It would have been impossible without her."

"Impossible, yes," he mumbled. He turned back to the knight. "Well, then!" he said at last, sitting upright in his saddle. "There's no need to be knocking about here in the country when we could be having celebrations back at the castle!"

A great cheer went up. Immediately, four of the strongest knights hoisted Rosetta, Prince Godric, Laurel and a somewhat unnerved Norbert Fangl on their shoulders, while King Walther gave Sylvie a hand up onto his horse.

Jouncing along down the road, the knights sang their terribly manly songs of victory while Sylvie held an overexcited Lulu in her arms. At the drawbridge, the guards presented arms. The king inclined his head and led the procession under the portcullis and into the castle courtyard.

Before long the festivities were in full swing. Queen Emmeline wept to see her Lulu again and was amazed at the little creature's new tricks.

"Where's Pingree?" she cried delightedly as Lulu executed a series of back flips. "He should work up an act with Lulu!"

"Yes," the king agreed. "Where is that fellow?"

The dog suddenly leapt from the queen's arms and scampered under the long table, emerging a moment later chasing a little green pig.

"How did *that* get in here?"

Laurel looked at the frantic animal, and then went over to the part of the floor where the story's text was imbedded.

"Interesting," she said, peering at a sentence about the jester. "You might take a look at this, Your Highness."

The king was aghast when he saw where she was pointing. He immediately called for the Chief Engineer and asked him to change some letters around.

So it was that the word, "Greenpig" was turned into "Pingree", at which moment the piglet tumbled snout over tail onto the floor and was human again. At least, he was Pingree again – a very out-of-sorts Pingree. It didn't help his mood to find that the entire court was whooping with laughter and clapping lustily.

"Do that again, Pingree!" shouted a courtier.

"Oink, oink!" cried a baroness in a hilarious soprano.

"You'll pay for this!" pouted the jester, stamping his little foot. "All of you!"

But the king beckoned him. "Come, come, we love thee well, Pingree. Come sit here by us."

"Well . . ."

"You'll be under my protection. I promise, no one will feed you acorns."

There was general laughter, but the jester was in better cheer. His mood improved even more when a pretty servant girl brought him sweet cake and a cup of grog.

Much later, while the sounds of laughter and singing still floated from the castle windows, Princess Sylvie strolled by the Mere with her friend, Laurel. They listened to the shushing of waves and breathed the night air. Sylvie tilted her head towards the moon.

"I hear that if the moon weren't so bright, we could see stars out there."

"That's right," Laurel said.

"Fangl says there are millions of them."

Laurel smiled and looked down.

"Wouldn't you like to see them?" said Sylvie. "Wouldn't you like to go to them?"

"Of course. At least," she said, "the part of me that is you would like to."

Sylvie looked at her sideways. "The part of me that is you," she repeated quietly. "Do you like that part of you?"

Laurel laughed and gave her a push. "Not when she's fishing for compliments!"

"I am not!"

"I'll race you to the point."

The girls took off along the sandy margin of the Mere, laughing and getting their shoes soaked, while overhead a full moon hung in the velvet sky like a picture in a lovely old book.

RODERICK TOWNLEY

THE GREAT GOOD THING

SEPTEMBER 2003

Sylvie is eternally twelve years old and has been a princess for more
than 80 years, ever since the novel she lives in was first published.
But she's getting bored and longs to break free of the never-ending
adventure. Then after many years of neglect the book is opened and,
as a new reader gazes down into Chapter One, Sylvie breaks an
important rule for all storybook characters - she looks at the Reader.
Worse still, she gets to know the Reader, a shy young girl called
Claire. And when Claire falls asleep with the book open, Sylvie
enters the girl's dreams and discovers a new and exciting world.
A world where adventures are rewritten daily, and dark, unpre-
dictable dangers lie in wait - and where Sylvie must achieve one
great, good thing to save the lives of everyone she loves.

ISBN 0 689 83714 3